He's safe!

The ball hit Hal's glove ⟨...⟩ *race for the bag, the tagging of the base, the catch, the turn, the throw—it all evaporated under the weight of the ball landing in his glove.*

Hal tried to complete the play anyway. He got the ball out of his glove with his right hand, turned off balance, and sent a soaring throw to first base. The seconds lost, first in Hal's recovery from the catch and then in his sailing throw, enabled Warner to win the race. He beat the throw to first.

Hal knew instantly what had happened. Freddie had given him a "heavy" throw—a "dead ball" with no spin. It had hung in the air a second too long and then dropped lifelessly.

And this "heavy" throw was no accident.

"As usual, Dygard is right on target with his sports details."   —*School Library Journal*

BY THE SAME AUTHOR

Backfield Package
Forward Pass
Game Plan
Halfback Tough
Outside Shooter
Point Spread
Quarterback Walk-on
Rebound Caper
The Rebounder
The Rookie Arrives
Running Scared
Soccer Duel
Tournament Upstart
Wilderness Peril
Winning Kicker

INFIELD HIT

THOMAS J. DYGARD

PUFFIN BOOKS

PUFFIN BOOKS
Published by the Penguin Group
Penguin Books USA Inc., 375 Hudson Street, New York, New York 10014, U.S.A.
Penguin Books Ltd, 27 Wrights Lane, London W8 5TZ, England
Penguin Books Australia Ltd, Ringwood, Victoria, Australia
Penguin Books Canada Ltd, 10 Alcorn Avenue, Toronto, Ontario, Canada M4V 3B2
Penguin Books (N.Z.) Ltd, 182-190 Wairau Road, Auckland 10, New Zealand

Penguin Books Ltd, Registered Offices: Harmondsworth, Middlesex, England

First published in the United States of America by
William Morrow and Company, Inc., 1995
Reprinted by arrangement with William Morrow and Company, Inc.
Published in Puffin Books, 1997

10 9 8 7 6 5 4 3 2 1

LIBRARY OF CONGRESS CATALOGING-IN-PUBLICATION DATA
Dygard, Thomas J.
Infield hit / Thomas J. Dygard.
p. cm.
Summary: After transferring to a new high school during his junior year,
Hal tries to make friends, gain a starting position on the baseball team,
and hide the fact that his dad is a famous ex-major leaguer.
ISBN 0-14-037935-5 (pbk.)
[1. Baseball—Fiction. 2. Moving, Household—Fiction.
3. Friendship—Fiction.] I. Title.
PZ7.D9893In 1997 [Fic]—dc20 96-38204 CIP AC

Printed in the United States of America

This book is dedicated to my wife,
Patty—no baseball fan,
but my best friend

INFIELD HIT

Chapter 1

ONE THING HAL STEVENS liked about his new school was that nobody there knew he was the son of Ralph Stevens, the now-retired legendary third baseman of the St. Louis Cardinals.

But that was about the only thing he liked.

Now in his third week, Hal arrived at Cannon City High each morning not knowing anyone. He'd sit through his classes, walk the hallways, and leave in the afternoon— still not knowing anyone.

But moving into unfamiliar territory, knowing no one, was nothing new to Hal. This was the third time he and his mother had moved since the divorce almost six years ago. First there had been Ames, Iowa, where they'd lived with his mother's parents while she worked toward a law degree at the university. Next had been Oklahoma City, for his mother's first job with her new law degree in hand. And now the move to Cannon City, in western Illinois, for a better job—director of labor relations at Walters Medical

Laboratory, on the northern outskirts of town.

"This will be the last move until you're out of high school," Ellen Stevens had said. "That's a promise. I know this has been tough on you."

Hal wondered if she really knew how tough.

By the time Hal appeared at Cannon City High in late February and registered for the second half of his junior year, all the guys had their own friends, their own groups. Each of his new teachers introduced him to the class, which embarrassed Hal. But it didn't really matter. Nobody was listening anyway.

For all his experience of moving into new neighborhoods and appearing at new schools, Hal still felt uncomfortable trying to make contact with classmates. Too often, it seemed, groups of friends did not feel the need for a new face. The result, as Hal knew only too well, could be cold rejection.

Maybe it was unintentional. That's what Hal always told himself. But that feeling of rejection was there anyway.

Sure, he was beginning to recognize some of the faces, and some of the students were starting to remember his name. Some of them nodded and smiled, and occasionally they said, "Hi." But by the time Hal returned the nod or the smile or the greeting, they had moved past him, heading off somewhere with their friends. Although some of them were friendly to the stranger, the new student remained a stranger.

From his first day at Cannon City High, Hal had consoled himself with the thought that springtime was coming and with it, baseball.

He was looking forward to the start of the season for more than just the fun of playing the game. His life would change when baseball started. He would be a member of the team. He would be one of the group. He would have friends.

Although Hal was not strong—he had the slender frame of his mother rather than the muscular physique of his father—he was a skillful fielder at third base. And, wielding a heavy bat, he got his share of extra-base hits.

Hal loved everything about baseball: the crack of the bat hitting the ball, the thump of the ball socking into the glove, the running, the fielding. He even loved just watching the game, just smelling the springtime air and the freshly mown grass that went with baseball.

After the divorce, when Hal and his mother moved from St. Louis to Ames, and then to Oklahoma City, he had felt the pain of leaving friends behind and the fears of facing strangers in an unknown piace. But at Blodgett High in Oklahoma City, he discovered that his love of baseball offered a solution to the problem. His teammates became his friends, and the Blodgett High baseball team became his crowd. Eventually students who weren't on the team, having seen him play, recognized him, and he began to form friendships outside of baseball. Then his mother announced the next move.

Hal was sure it would be the same at Cannon City High: friendships through baseball.

But with a difference this time. For as long as he could keep the secret, nobody was going to know that Hal was the son of the famous Ralph Stevens.

At Blodgett High, Hal's best friends on the team knew that his father was Ralph Stevens—he had told them—and it was no big deal.

No big deal, that is, until the word started getting around. Then people he hardly knew began to gawk at him. Some of his own teammates seemed to be in awe of him. Opposing players pointed him out to friends. Occasionally teachers commented on Hal's famous father.

And then, worst of all, the local newspaper sent a reporter to a couple of the Blodgett High games to write a story about "the son of Ralph Stevens." It was embarrassing when the reporter wrote that Hal had neither his father's strong throwing arm at third base nor his father's sure control of a big bat at the plate.

So this time, Hal Stevens was going to be just Hal Stevens. Period. Nobody was going to know otherwise, if he could help it.

4

And that included the coach—especially the coach.

Hal had been surprised, and a bit alarmed, when he arrived at Cannon City High and discovered that the baseball coach was Don Mavis, the same Don Mavis who played shortstop for twelve years in the National League, first for Atlanta and then for Los Angeles. Now retired, Don Mavis had returned to his home area of western Illinois and was living on a farm thirty miles north of Cannon City. He had agreed to coach the team—for one year only, he specified—when the former coach abruptly departed at midterm to pursue a professional baseball career. Cannon City High had been faced with an emergency, until someone on the school board had a brainstorm and a committee went calling on Don Mavis at his farm.

"Do you know him?" Hal had asked his mother when he found out who his baseball coach would be.

"I've met him," she had said. "But, no, I don't really know him. He never played on a team with your father, you know. I met him once or twice at All-Star games, that's all."

"Dad knew him, then?"

"Oh, yes."

Well, Hal had concluded, there are lots of people in the world named Stevens. Probably Don Mavis would never think to compare the throwing arms and batting powers of Hal Stevens and Ralph Stevens.

Hal knew that his secret couldn't last forever. His

mother would mention her ex-husband to someone at Walters Medical, or someone would ask and she would reply that, yes, she had been married to the famous third baseman. Then, naturally, that someone at Walters Medical would go home and tell the family. The family, of course, would include a Cannon City High student. Then the news would circulate through the halls and everyone would know. Hal knew it was certain to happen one day.

But until that day came, Hal Stevens was going to be just Hal Stevens, not the son of Ralph Stevens.

He was going to play baseball without anyone gaping at him, without any reporter comparing him with his father. And he was, at last, going to make some real friends at a new school.

Coming out of American history class at noon, the boy in front of Hal said to a friend, "Has anyone ever met or even seen Don Mavis? He ought to be showing up around the school, shouldn't he?"

Hal had been in the classroom with the boy for three weeks, so he knew his last name was Patterson, but he didn't know his first name. The American history teacher, Mr. Henderson, always referred to his students as Mister So-and-So. The other boy's name was Hart, but Hal didn't know his first name, either.

The boy named Hart replied, "No reason for him to

6

show up until practice starts, is there? He's not a teacher—just the baseball coach, you know."

As they moved into the corridor, Hal stepped up until he was even with the two boys and asked, "Are you baseball players?"

Both of them turned to Hal with questioning looks on their faces. Hal had never exchanged a word with either of them, and here he was injecting himself into their conversation. For a moment, he was sorry he had spoken.

Then the boy named Patterson grinned and said, "I'm a baseball player, but there's some question about Jason here."

Hal smiled back and almost audibly sighed in relief.

He glanced at the other boy. Okay, he said to himself, it's Jason. Jason Hart.

Jason jabbed the boy named Patterson with an elbow.

Hal said, "You're, uh...Patterson?"

"Ed. And you're Mr. Stevens."

"Hal," he said. "So nobody's met Don Mavis yet?"

"Not yet," Ed said, "and everybody is kind of anxious."

"I guess."

"Heck, I never even seen a major-league ball player, much less played for one."

Hal felt like rolling his eyes to the ceiling, but he said nothing.

"You play baseball?" Jason asked.

"Yeah. Third base."

"Uh-oh," Ed said.

"What?"

"Blaine Wilkins is a senior, and this is his third year as a starter. He's sort of got a lock on the third-base job."

Before Hal could reply, Jason said, "There's Rich." He waved and called to a lanky boy down the hallway.

The boy turned and waved back, and Ed and Jason moved ahead to catch up with him.

Hal walked on alone toward the cafeteria.

Chapter 2

ON SIGN-UP DAY, HAL fell in step with Jason as they came out of their last class, a first-year French course. Hal's head was still swimming with the problem he was having with his accent. They stopped at their lockers, picked up their gym bags, and headed down the hall toward the stairs.

"At last," Jason said, "we get to meet the great Don Mavis."

In the last few days leading up to the start of practice, Hal had seen the excitement build among the few boys he knew to be baseball players—Ed, Jason, Rich, and a couple of others.

"Yep," Hal said, feeling a mix of the same excitement Jason was experiencing and a nervousness that was his alone.

Was Don Mavis going to know—somehow, some way—that Hal was the son of Ralph Stevens, and announce it when they met?

Hal and Jason hurried down the steps, turned the corner, and walked down the shadowy hallway. Ahead of them, Hal saw Ed turning in to the locker room. Ed waved and Hal and Jason waved back.

Hal and Jason walked on to the door, and Hal followed Jason in.

Don Mavis was standing at the end of a table, greeting the incoming players with an introductory handshake and a friendly smile. The boy behind the table holding a sign-up clipboard and handing out uniforms was a familiar face from the corridors, but Hal did not know his name.

Jason stepped forward, but Hal paused a moment and studied the man who had played next to his father in All-Star games. They had also played against each other in dozens of games through the years when both infielders were standouts in the National League. Don Mavis was wearing slacks, a sports shirt, and a heavy-knit sweater. He looked fit enough to play in an All-Star game right now, even though he had retired from baseball several years ago. His boyish appearance surprised Hal. Don Mavis had an unlined face and light blue eyes. His light red hair, cut short and combed to the side, fell a bit over his forehead, and a cowlick stood up in the back. He had the open, friendly face and relaxed smile of a man perfectly at ease.

Well, Hal thought, what did you expect?

A boy Hal didn't know was giving the boy with the clipboard all the information required—name, height, weight, position—and then moving away with a basket containing his uniform. He glanced at Hal and walked on.

Hal walked over and waited for Jason to finish with Don Mavis. Then he was standing in front of the man and saying, "Coach Mavis, I'm Hal Stevens."

Coach Mavis looked Hal in the eye a moment, then gave him his easy smile and said, "Hello, Hal, I'm pleased to meet you." They shook hands. "Sign up, and Jerry will issue you a uniform."

He did not add, "You're the son of Ralph Stevens, aren't you?"

On the field, under dark clouds threatening a spring shower, Coach Mavis called the players around him in the area between the bench and the third-base line.

His glove thrust into his hip pocket, Hal was standing next to Ed Patterson. Ed was nervously punching his left fist into his huge first-baseman's mitt.

Coach Mavis began speaking. "It's good to be back in baseball," he said. He was smiling in sort of a shy way now, and he seemed uncomfortable being the center of attention. "I'm looking forward to the season."

Hal liked the way Don Mavis put it. The physical education teacher who had been the coach at Blodgett High had always issued orders and demanded immediate compliance. But this former All-Star shortstop was putting the Cannon City Gunners on his level. Everyone on the field was a baseball player—Don Mavis, Hal Stevens, Ed Patterson, everyone.

"You can tell he doesn't have any experience as a coach," Ed whispered with a grin on his face.

"What do you mean?"

"He's nice."

Hal smiled.

Ed added, "Coach Burroughs was a jerk."

But after Coach Mavis put the players through stretching exercises and a loosening-up jog around the field, he underwent a personality change. Gone was the relaxed manner; now he was as taut as a violin string. There was no more of the warm smile; now he frowned and scowled. The boyishness was still there—maybe he couldn't shake it—but now he was intensely serious. Hal thought he was seeing the concentration and competitiveness that made a friendly, easygoing man into an All-Star shortstop. Don Mavis was taking on the same expression of intensity that Hal had seen on his father's face so many times.

When Hal and the others took their swings at the plate, Coach Mavis stood behind the batting screen and watched like an umpire, slightly bent, hands on knees. He squinted at the action in front of him and said nothing.

Hal did not do well in his first turn at the plate. The pitcher, Rich Oliver, had a fastball that hummed. Hal had seen few pitchers last season in Oklahoma City with Rich's speed. Hal, using a heavy bat for extra clout, swung clumsily and missed the first two pitches. On the third, he got a piece of the ball and fouled it off behind the screen. At the finish of his turn he had made only one really good connection, sending a screaming liner into left center field. In sum, not good.

As he left the batter's box, Hal glanced at Don Mavis. The coach was already frowning at the next batter, Jason Hart.

When the infielders were gobbling up grounders and firing the ball across to Ed at first base, Coach Mavis stood first at the third-base line and then at the first-base line and watched without expression, his hands thrust into the hip pockets of his slacks. Again, he said nothing. He just watched and frowned. And it was the same when the coach walked down the foul lines and watched the outfielders gathering in high flies and racing after line drives.

Through the first practice session Hal slowly began putting more names with faces and assigning them positions on the team. There had been no introduction, either in the locker room or in the brief meeting on the field before practice. Everybody was new to Coach Mavis, of course, and maybe the coach assumed that all the boys knew one another. Most of them did, it seemed to Hal. As far as he could tell, he was the only new player on the team except for some boys up from junior high for their first season—and they had been attending Cannon City High since school opened last September.

Hal had no trouble identifying his competition for third base. At the start of the infield drill, Coach Mavis said simply, "Where we've got two players at the same position, swap out—take turns fielding the hits."

The boy alternating with Hal looked older—Ed had said Blaine Wilkins was a senior—and he certainly looked stronger. He paid no attention to Hal.

After the second grounder to third base—a bouncer that Hal gloved easily, then lofted across to Ed at first base—he stepped back for Blaine to take his turn and said, "I'm Hal Stevens."

Blaine looked at Hal as if seeing him for the first time. For a moment, Hal thought he wasn't going to respond at all. Then he said, "Blaine Wilkins." That was all, just his name. Then he focused on the batter sending a grounder to the shortstop.

For the rest of the drill, Hal watched Blaine closely. He always got a good jump on the ball, and he had a sure glove hand, whether spearing a line drive or going after a grounder. Plus, he had a strong right arm that rifled the ball across the diamond with authority.

Blaine, while ignoring Hal, kept up an atta-boy and way-to-go line of chatter whenever the shortstop, a boy named Freddie, or the second baseman, whose name was

14

Warner, made a play. And Freddie and Warner cheered Blaine in return—but not Hal.

Hal shrugged. So the infielders were all good friends. And Hal? He was, well, an outsider.

When Hal came out the front door of the school, both the wide steps and the manicured lawn that spread out to the street were empty. Except for students going out for baseball or track, everyone had left two hours before.

The early evening of this late March day was cool. Hal wore a jacket zipped to the neck, and he was glad of its warmth. But the first signs of spring were everywhere, as befitted the first day of baseball practice. The snow was long gone, and the color green was replacing it. Only the approaching darkness was a reminder that the short days of winter were a recent thing.

Hal turned to the left for the two-block walk to Ridgeway Avenue, where he would catch a bus for home.

Ahead of him, he saw a car across the intersection with four boys in it. Blaine Wilkins was at the wheel. Hal recognized the boy in the front seat next to Blaine as Warner, the second baseman. He could not identify the two boys in the backseat, but felt sure they were baseball players catching a ride home with Blaine. Remembering the shouts of encouragement for Blaine in the infield, he guessed one of the other riders probably was the shortstop, Freddie.

As he walked to Ridgeway Avenue, waited for a bus, and then boarded it and stared out at the darkening street, Hal felt a gloomy mood settle in. Yes, baseball season had finally arrived. He was playing, enjoying again the feel of the earth under his cleats, the cracking sound of the bat hitting the ball, the thump of his glove stopping a line drive. But one day of practice had told him that he was not going to beat out Blaine Wilkins at third base. The senior was more experienced, besides being a good fielder and a strong thrower. He wasn't bad as a hitter, either.

He had been lucky, Hal concluded, to have won the starting third-base position at Blodgett High as a sophomore. But Blodgett High was a small school. There hadn't been a lot of competition. Cannon City High was larger, and it had Blaine Wilkins to play third base.

Hal let himself in the front door of the apartment and called out, "I'm home."

"I'm in here," his mother said from the kitchen.

He walked into his bedroom and dropped his books on his bed. Then he took off his jacket and tossed that on the bed, too.

As he walked into the kitchen, his mother asked, "How'd it go?" Ellen Stevens was wearing jeans, a sweatshirt, and sneakers, as she always did after a day at the office in a suit.

"Okay, I guess," Hal said.

"I thought for a while today it was going to rain on your first practice."

"No, it didn't rain."

"You met Don Mavis, at last."

Hal climbed onto a stool at the counter separating the kitchen from the dining area. "Yes."

"How was he?"

"He seemed nice, real nice—until we got on the practice field."

"Oh?" His mother was asking a question, but her half-smiling expression seemed to say that she already knew the answer.

"You know, all friendly when we were signing up. And then, when we got on the field, real serious."

"Strictly business," she said.

"I guess so."

"Did you say anything about your father?"

Hal looked up at his mother. "No, I didn't."

Ellen's right eyebrow went up slightly, as it always did when she was a little surprised. She said nothing for a moment. Then when Hal offered no elaboration, she said, "Well, yes, I guess that's the best thing."

Chapter 3

IN THE DAYS THAT followed, Don Mavis made it clear that he considered baseball a game to be played and not a drill to be repeated.

Each day, after stretching exercises, the jogging, the fielding warmup, and the batting practice, Coach Mavis divided the squad into two teams for a game of three or four innings.

The pitchers worked one inning each and then usually went into some other position where the Cannon City Gunners didn't have a second player.

For Hal, it was an abrupt change from the style of the Blodgett High coach. He had had the players work incessantly on the technical skills of their positions—pepper games for infielders, one long fly after another for outfielders, practice throws to a catcher for the pitchers—with the thrill of actually playing left only to the scheduled games.

Hal loved the change. He was playing third base every

day, fielding real hits, with a real runner trying to beat the throw to first base. He was swinging at pitches with a real team of fielders watching him.

But Blaine Wilkins was playing third base every day, too. He was fielding real hits—fielding them as well as Hal. And he was rifling the ball across the diamond to beat a runner. His throwing arm was more powerful than Hal's, and more accurate on the long throw. Blaine was not as quick as Hal, but Hal had to admit that Blaine was quick enough.

At the plate, Blaine hit the ball hard—not as hard as Warner Dawson, a real slugger, or Ed Patterson, but he was a consistently strong hitter. Frequently his shots were line drives into the outfield, the stuff that doubles are made of.

As the end of the first week of practice approached, Hal was unable to escape the fact that every good play he made in the field was not quite as good as Blaine's last good play. And Blaine was belting the ball out of the infield twice for every time Hal managed to bring his big bat around and make a good connection.

Hal was sure that Coach Mavis was seeing the difference—he didn't seem to miss anything. He wandered the field during the hitting and fielding drills that opened each session, standing and staring, occasionally offering a comment. When the intrasquad innings got under way, he took a seat on the bench and watched. Sometimes between innings he offered a comment to a player. But mostly he kept quiet, just watching. No, Hal had no doubts that the coach was seeing the differences between the two third basemen.

Blaine showed that he was noticing, too. No longer pointedly ignoring the slender newcomer who wanted his third-base job, he now glanced at Hal after making a good play in the field, gave a little nod, and seemed to be saying, "See that?" Hal caught himself looking away to avoid the glance and the nod.

Even Blaine's friends, Freddie Harrison and Warner Dawson, were quieting down. They no longer shouted their congratulations whenever Blaine made a good play. There was no need to: In less than a week of practice, Blaine obviously had won the third-base job. No doubt about it.

On Thursday evening, Hal's mother greeted his arrival home with a question: "What's wrong?"

Hal frowned and wished for the thousandth time that his mother was not so good at reading his mind. "Who says anything is wrong?"

"Your face looks like a thundercloud. Did something happen?"

Hal looked at the ceiling.

"Come on, out with it," she said.

Hal took a deep breath. "I haven't got a chance in the world of starting at third base." As he said the words, he wondered if his father had ever had to say anything like that when he was in high school. Probably not, he thought, and the conclusion did not help his mood. "No chance," he added.

"Did Coach Mavis tell you?"

"He doesn't have to."

"Well, nothing is settled until the lineup is posted, is it?"

How could his mother always be so hopeful? "I guess not," he finally said, giving up.

But Ellen Stevens wasn't giving up. She did something at the stove, then turned back to him. "You just keep on doing the best you can and things will work out. Mark my words."

Hal gave her a little smile that he did not feel like giving and said, "Sure."

At least so far no one knew that it was the son of Ralph Stevens who was losing the battle for third base.

The next morning, calculus and American history kept Hal's mind off baseball. In all his classes, he was feeling the burden of having arrived at Cannon City High in the middle of the school year. Now, at the end of his fifth week, he was finally beginning to make a bit of progress. He could feel it. But there was still more catching up to do in this new curriculum with a new set of teachers and different textbooks.

At noon, he dropped off his books in his locker and walked toward the cafeteria. He reflected that next Friday—one week from today—was the first scheduled game of the season for the Cannon City Gunners. Well, he thought, he'd be watching from the bench.

In the cafeteria Hal moved through the line and stopped with his tray in his hands, looking for a friendly face to join. He spotted Blaine, Freddie, and Warner seated together at the end of a long table, but he did not need their company and was sure they did not want his. He saw Jason seated across from a girl, talking seriously, and decided not to barge in.

All through the cafeteria he saw faces that were familiar from classrooms and the hallways—faces mostly without names. Everybody was with somebody, one of a group of friends. He did not see any other baseball players.

He knew what his mother would say: "Walk over and sit down with someone and introduce yourself. That's the way you get to meet people."

Hal wished it were that easy. He could not bring himself to do it.

Then Ed's voice came at him from behind. "Are you going to eat here, standing up, or do you want to find a table?"

Hal turned and looked into Ed's smiling face with a sense of relief. "There's a couple of spots," he said, and led the way to the table.

When they were seated, Ed said, "Have you noticed that Coach Mavis watches you a lot?"

Hal was surprised. Then, with a slight twinge of alarm, he wondered if Don Mavis had learned somehow that he was Ralph Steven's son. Finally, he shrugged. "Coach Mavis watches everyone a lot. I've noticed that."

"No, really, he's always watching you." Ed leaned forward, eyeing Hal. "He lets me play first base and hardly pays any attention. He lets Freddie run around at shortstop. He doesn't seem to notice Warner clumping around at second base, bobbling half the balls hit to him. But you—every time you catch the ball, every time you swing at the plate, he's staring at you."

Hal managed a small grin. "He's probably trying to figure out where to seat me on the bench this season."

Ed took a bite and nodded his head. "Uh-huh. Blaine's pretty good," he said. "There's no getting around it."

"And that leaves me on the bench, watching instead of playing."

"Well, Blaine's a senior and you're a junior, so maybe..."

"Coach Mavis is only in the job for one year, remember, so he's not thinking about next year."

"I sat on the bench last year. I got into some games as

a pinch hitter, but that's all. Now I'm the only first base-man we've got. It was worth the wait."

"I guess that's what I'll do this year—wait."

"Yeah, maybe. But he's watching you. He looks at you in a different way."

Hal gave Ed a sharp glance, then shrugged.

Maybe Ed was right.

Hal, changing into his uniform for practice, remembered the times he had gobbled up a grounder at third base, made the throw to first, and then turned to see Don Mavis watching him. The coach had had a different kind of look on his face, almost quizzical. Hal remembered the times at bat, whether striking out or connecting with his heavy bat for a long fly, when he had looked up to see Coach Mavis studying him. He'd always assumed that the coach, who seldom said anything—just watched—was giv-ing every player the same silent gaze. But now that he thought about it, he began to think that maybe it wasn't the same gaze.

Hal finished tying his shoelaces and straightened up. Unconsciously, he shook his head. This was all his imagi-nation. He wasn't seeing anything different in the way the coach looked at him. He couldn't be. And Ed was mis-taken. He had to be. The fact remained that Blaine was the better third baseman. No question. And that left Hal on the bench. So what was there for the coach to watch? Hal grabbed his glove out of the locker and headed to the playing field.

During the intrasquad innings Coach Mavis sat on the bench, as always, leaning forward, elbows on knees, hands clasped, watching the hitters and the fielders without comment.

Hal felt the coach's eyes on him every time he caught the ball and cocked his arm for the long throw to first base. At bat, he knew the coach was watching. But, Hal told himself, the coach was watching every player catching the ball or throwing it. He was staring at every hitter.

A light rain began falling with two out in the bottom of the third inning. Coach Mavis stood up, looked at the sky, and called an end to the practice session.

Hal, in the field, began walking toward the back door of the school. It had not been a good day for him. He had gone hitless in two trips to the plate, striking out one time and bouncing out to second the other time. He had fielded four chances flawlessly, but Jason had beat out a hit to third when Hal, off balance and starting the throw from low near the ground, sent the ball sailing in a high arc to Ed's glove at first base.

Ahead of him, Hal saw Coach Mavis peel Warner away from Blaine and Freddie. He said something and Warner nodded and walked the rest of the way in with the coach.

Hal figured he knew what was happening. Warner had

bobbled one grounder and let a line drive bounce off his glove. Maybe Coach Mavis didn't think that Warner's booming home run in the first inning made up for his errors in the field and was going to tell him so.

In the locker room, Hal quickly stripped off his uniform and headed for the showers. He was the first one in, and he turned on a shower and stood for a moment enjoying the needles of hot water. Then he lathered and rinsed and stepped out, grabbing a towel and wrapping it around his waist. By that time, other players were entering the showers.

Warner walked into the locker room a few minutes later, wearing a grim expression. Coach Mavis must have been pretty tough on him. Warner did not speak to or even look at Hal as he passed. Hal did not speak, either.

Hal was almost dressed, stuffing his shirttail into his jeans, when Don Mavis appeared at his side.

"Hal, stop in and see me a minute in the coaches' office before you leave, would you?"

Chapter 4

HAL, WITH HIS JACKET on and his books held in his right hand, stepped into the open doorway of the coaches' office.

The room was large, with five metal desks scattered about, each with one or two file cabinets on one side and an extra chair on the other. The walls seemed to be covered with bulletin boards laden with thumbtacked sheets of paper.

Coach Mavis was seated at a desk at the far end of the room. "Come in, Hal," he said, getting to his feet. He was the friendly, almost boyish Don Mavis of sign-up day, not the stern and watchful tutor of the practice field. He was smiling. "Have a seat," he said, gesturing at the chair alongside his desk.

Only one other desk in the room was occupied at this late hour. The other man undoubtedly was a coach, but Hal did not know him. He continued what he was doing without looking up.

Coach Mavis sat down and leaned back, propping a foot on an open drawer. "Hal, why do you play third base?"

The question caught Hal by surprise. He knew the answer, of course. He had always played third base. For the son of Ralph Stevens, third base was the only position to play. He had a clear memory of his father once introducing him to the players at spring practice as "my little third baseman"—and the memory jumped through his brain now. Hal Stevens had wanted to be a third baseman almost before he could walk. But that wasn't the answer he wanted to give to Don Mavis. He said, "Because I like playing third base."

Coach Mavis smiled and said, almost casually, "You really haven't got the arm for third base, you know."

Hal sat, hardly breathing. Was the coach giving him formal notice that he had lost out to Blaine? Well, Hal already knew that. It was obvious to everyone. He did not need to be told that Blaine was the better third baseman. So what was the point of this meeting?

In a brief moment of panic he thought that perhaps the coach was telling him that he was wasting his time trying out for the team at all, and that he ought to forget baseball. But that couldn't be it. Hal knew he was a quick and sure-handed fielder. He knew that when he was able to put the heavy bat on a pitch, the ball took a long trip. Then what did Coach Mavis mean?

28

Hal said, "I know I haven't got the strongest arm in the world, but...," and he let the sentence trail off.

"You've got all the other tools —good hands, good footwork, quickness." Coach Mavis spoke softly, matter-of-factly, with none of the intensity he showed on the practice field. He was relaxed and did not move as he spoke. "But your throwing arm is a disadvantage at third base."

Hal saw no point in protesting. He knew the coach was right. He finally said, "I guess so."

Don Mavis nodded slightly at Hal's agreement and said, "On Monday, I want you to start working at second base."

"Second base," Hal said, almost to himself. He saw the face of Warner Dawson, a senior, the returning starter at second base, a heavy hitter. Hal could no more beat out Warner Dawson than he could beat out Blaine Wilkins. If he was going to ride the bench, what difference did it make which position was listed alongside his name?

Coach Mavis continued, as if Hal had not spoken. "It's a shorter throw to first base. The lack of a strong throwing arm is less a handicap at second—hardly a handicap at all, as a matter of fact. And, as I said, you've got the other tools—good hands, quickness. What do you say?"

Hal frowned. He kept thinking, But I've always been a third baseman. Yet, Coach Mavis's arguments made sense.

Maybe he would be better at second base. And, when it came to winning a position, losing out to Warner was no worse than losing out to Blaine. He said, "Okay, sure."

Coach Mavis smiled again. "Good. I think with a little time to orient yourself in the new position, you're going to make a fine second baseman."

Was the coach saying that Hal had a chance of starting at second base? Hal did not speak the question, but the expression on his face must have given it away.

Coach Mavis said, "I'm moving Warner to right field. We need to keep his heavy hitting in the lineup, but we need better glove work at second base."

The picture of the coach walking off the practice field with Warner flashed through Hal's mind, followed by the vision of an angry Warner Dawson entering the locker room later. Hal had thought Coach Mavis was rebuking Warner for his fumbles. But the coach had brought him into this office and told him that he was being moved to right field. Maybe the coach had also told Warner that he was putting the quick-footed newcomer with the sure hands in his place at second base. Or maybe Warner had guessed that Hal Stevens was going to replace him.

To Coach Mavis, Hal said only, "I see."

Hal started to get to his feet, but Don Mavis, his foot still propped up on the open drawer, made no move to get up. Hal settled back in the chair.

30

"There's one other thing, Hal," he said.

"Yes?" He waited, with the scary thought in the back of his mind that Coach Mavis somehow knew he was the son of Ralph Stevens and was going to say so.

"I want you to throw away that club you've been using for a bat. It's so heavy you can hardly drag it to the plate, much less swing it at a pitch."

"But it's—"

Coach Mavis smiled. "I know, I know," he said. "The heavy bat gives you more wallop when you hit the ball, doesn't it?"

"Yes."

"Trouble is, you don't hit the ball often enough because you can't swing the bat smoothly. Warner swings a big bat. So does Ed. They're strong enough to handle a heavy bat. You aren't. Get yourself a bat you can handle and learn to place your hits. An infield single is better than a long fly for an out any day of the week."

Hal nodded, frowning slightly. He knew that Coach Mavis was right. But he also knew that Ralph Stevens had swung a heavy bat. He had been a power hitter, batting fifth in the lineup. He remembered, from years ago, seeing his father's heavily muscled shoulders and arms bring the big bat around, smashing a line drive toward the fence. In fact, he had one of those bats at home. His father had given it to him when Hal was barely able to lift it. Ralph

Stevens had said, "Don't worry. You'll be able to use it one of these days."

"You've got the speed for it—the speed needed to beat out an infield hit, or a bunt," Coach Mavis was saying. "I haven't timed anyone, but I'd bet you're the fastest base-path runner on the team." With a smile he added, "It's a shame to waste that speed on strikeouts and high flies to the outfield."

Hal returned the smile but did not speak.

"Okay?" Coach Mavis prompted.

"Okay."

Coach Mavis watched Hal for a moment and then said, "You're going to have to work at it. This is going to be an entirely different style of hitting for you. No more winding up and swinging from the heels, praying that you connect. More likely, you're going to be doing more bunting. You're going to have to learn to pick your shots and poke the ball where you want it to go. It's not easy, so I really do mean you'll have to work at it. Hitting is an art form, and like any art form, it takes practice to become good."

Hal nodded. "I'll work on it," he said.

Hal and Coach Mavis both stood. Hal said, "Thanks."

Coach Mavis grinned. "You're welcome."

The hallway was empty, but the lights were still on in the locker room when Hal walked by the door. He glanced in as he passed. Had the coach told Warner that Hal was taking over second base? If so, had Warner told any of the players? Had he even told anyone he was being shifted to right field? The last of the players were pulling on their clothes. Hal spotted a pitcher, Rich Oliver. Then he walked on.

He was barely conscious of his walk to the bus stop. All he could think was, I'm going to be a starter. I'm not going to spend the season sitting on the bench. I'm going to play in the games.

At home, he unlocked the front door and threw it open, ready to shout, but all was heavy shadows, the semi-darkness of early evening. He felt for the wall switch and found it, then turned on the lights and closed the door.

Where was his mother?

She was always here when he arrived home in the late afternoon from practice. Before baseball started, he had beaten her home, but not by much. Maybe half an hour, an hour. The workday started and ended early at Walters Medical.

He frowned and wondered if he should worry. Maybe there had been a car accident. Or—something else. Perhaps she'd been taken ill, was in a hospital.

He thought of calling her office. But, no, everyone would be gone at this late hour. Maybe he should call the police; they'd know if there had been an accident. Or maybe he should call the hospitals.

Hal stood still for a moment. He told himself not to

panic. He'd had this fear before, sometimes at the weirdest times and places, ever since the divorce. Beyond his concern for his mother, he feared for himself if something should happen to her. He lived with his mother, and his mother only. What if something happened to her? He'd be alone. Where would he go? Probably to live with his father and Gloria.

Hal's father lived with his second wife in an apartment in Manhattan and worked with an advertising agency, traveling all over the country lining up celebrity athletes for endorsements. That would leave Hal with Gloria most of the time. Gloria was okay, or at least seemed so whenever he visited, but she was not his mother.

The ringing of the telephone startled him, and he jumped. He moved over and picked up the receiver, wondering if he was about to hear bad news. "Hello."

"Hal?"

It was not his mother's voice, and he felt his heart skip a beat.

"Yes."

"This is your mother's secretary, Helen Michaels."

Again his heartbeat skipped.

"Yes."

"I've been trying to reach you every ten minutes. Your mother is tied up in a meeting and won't be home for at least another hour. She says to tell you to wait, and she'll pick up a pizza for dinner."

Hal released his breath. "Thank you," he said.

He hung up the telephone and walked into his room. He dropped his books on his desk, removed his jacket, and laid it on the bed. Then he walked across to a bookshelf and extracted a large, thin book with a bright red cover. The title was *How to Play Baseball*. He had almost memorized the chapter on playing third base. He had even, with the door to his room closed, practiced in the mirror striking the poses of the third baseman in the pictures.

Now he turned to the chapter on playing second base.

The pizza was a treat for Hal. His mother didn't often serve pizza, or other fast foods like hamburgers with fries, hot dogs, or tacos.

"So, it looks like we're having pizza as a celebration," she said after he told her his news. "I told you, didn't I, that if you kept doing your best, things would work out."

After dinner, Hal telephoned Ed Patterson and caught him just before he left for a party. No, Hal said, he hadn't been invited. He did not even know the person Ed named as the host. He thought for a moment that Ed might say, "Why don't you go with me, it'll be all right." But Ed didn't.

Then Hal told Ed about his meeting with Coach Mavis. Ed said nothing for a moment, which puzzled Hal. Why wasn't Ed happy for him? Then he said only,

"Ummm." Hal frowned into the phone and waited. Then Ed said, "That's great."

But Ed didn't make it sound great, so Hal asked, "What's the matter?"

"That explains why Warner was stomping around the locker room and going into a huddle with Blaine and Freddie, then all of them being mad."

"He's not being benched. What's there to be mad about?"

"Well, the three of them have played together in the infield the last two years. I guess they figured they had a lock on it this year, especially with the way Blaine was beating you out at third base. Maybe Warner was a little embarrassed, too."

"Uh-huh. I see."

"Don't worry about it. It's Coach Mavis's decision, no fault of yours."

Hal frowned again. That was a funny way of putting it.

"Got to run," Ed said suddenly. "My ride is here."

Hal hesitated before mentioning his second reason for phoning Ed. Then he plunged ahead. "Just a second, huh? The reason I called—"

"Yeah?"

"Are you busy tomorrow morning?"

"No. Why?"

"Coach Mavis says I've got to start using a lighter bat

36

and learn how to place my hits, and I thought maybe you'd help me work on it."

Ed did not answer immediately, and Hal was suddenly sorry he had asked. Maybe he was pushing too hard. Maybe Ed was a better friend of Warner Dawson than Hal knew. But Ed liked to play baseball, and that was all Hal was asking, really.

"Sure," Ed said finally.

Hal felt a sense of relief, and then was embarrassed by the feeling. What was wrong about asking a teammate to meet and work on hitting? He said, "Good. At the school, about nine-thirty?"

"Right. I've really got to run."

Hal hung up the phone, wondering which of the nameless faces in the corridor was throwing a party without inviting the newcomer at Cannon City High.

Chapter 5

THE DRIZZLING RAIN THAT had cut short practice on Friday afternoon had blown away during the night, and the weather on Saturday morning was bright, clear, and crisp.

Hal, with a baseball in his jacket pocket and a bat in his hand, boarded the bus that would take him to Cannon City High.

He was hoping to find someone on hand at the school to let him in, and someone who would authorize his use of a basket of baseballs and a slimmer, lighter bat. But if the school was locked up tight, or there was nobody inside willing to let him borrow baseballs and a bat, he knew he would have to make do with what he had—one baseball and an oversized bat.

Seated on the almost-empty bus, Hal lifted the bat slightly and had to admit that Coach Mavis was right: It was too heavy for him. He wished he'd been thinking quickly enough yesterday to ask Coach Mavis to arrange for a bat and balls to use today. But Hal had been home before the thought of calling Ed for a workout occurred to him. And the coach was surely home on his farm for the weekend.

Hal stepped off the bus and walked the two blocks to the school. From the front, the building appeared closed and deserted. He tried the front door and found it locked. So he walked around the side to the back of the building.

Not only was the back door unlocked, but there seemed to Hal to be a surprising amount of activity for a Saturday morning. The lights were on in the hall, and the door was open to the large coaches' office. Hal could hear voices coming from inside.

He walked to the doorway and looked in. Several coaches or physical education instructors were there. Don Mavis was not among them.

Hal walked along the corridor to the equipment room. The door was locked.

He returned to the coaches' office and looked from one face to another. Finally, one of the men said, "Need something?"

"Coach Mavis isn't around, is he?" Hal asked, even though he was sure he wasn't. But the question seemed a good way to begin.

"No, he's not. Haven't seen him today."

Hal swallowed and plunged ahead. "I wanted to check out a bat and some balls."

"Check 'em out? What?"

"I have to practice my hitting. I've got a friend, Ed Patterson, coming to throw to me. I need a bat and some balls."

The coach looked skeptical. "Has Coach Mavis authorized this?"

"No, I haven't talked to him."

The coach glanced at the other people in the room, then returned his gaze to Hal. He didn't seem to know what to do.

"Look," Hal said, "I'll sign for everything, and I'll be responsible." Then he added, "I'm sure Coach Mavis would say okay, if he was here."

"You're on the baseball team?"

"Yes."

The coach took a breath, then said, "I guess it'll be all right, if you'll make sure everything is returned."

Hal sat cross-legged on the grass at the edge of the field, just beyond first base, and waited for Ed. To his right was a basket containing twenty baseballs, counted out one by one by the coach. To his left lay the slender bat that he had selected after hefting several in the equipment room.

A bit of the early springtime chill of western Illinois was in the air. Hal was glad he had worn a jacket instead of just a sweater.

He looked at his wristwatch. Nine-twenty. He told Ed

nine-thirty. No need to worry yet. But he did. Too many times in Ames and then in Oklahoma City he had been let down by new acquaintances he thought were going to be friends. Maybe Ed had changed his mind. Maybe, at the party last night, he had found something more attractive to do today.

Hal began to doubt the wisdom of having called Ed in the first place. Ed had acted a little funny when Hal made his request. Maybe Ed didn't really want to do it. Or maybe he'd thought about it later and decided not to come.

Hal looked at his watch again. Going on toward nine-twenty-five. Well, Hal had told Ed "about nine-thirty." That meant maybe a few minutes before or after.

Hal decided that if nine-thirty came and Ed was still nowhere in sight, he would not give up. So Ed was a few minutes late. Maybe Ed was one of those people who were always late. Hal told himself that he would wait until ten o'clock. But, he resolved, no later. Then, if Ed hadn't shown, he would return the baseballs and the bat to the equipment room and go home.

In the distance, a car went by on the street beyond left field. Hal recognized it as the one he'd seen Blaine and his friends riding in a few days ago. He squinted, trying to make out the occupants. Was Ed in the car? That was a weird thought, but it pcpped into his mind anyway. Hal couldn't see well enough at that distance to tell. The car moved on out of sight.

Hal turned and looked back past the school building toward the street leading to the bus stop on Ridgeway Avenue. Maybe Ed was riding the bus, like Hal had. He saw no one.

He was about to check his watch a third time when he heard the double beep of a car horn to his right. On the street beyond the edge of right field a car was pulling to the curb and coming to a halt.

Hal scrambled to his feet and started to wave.

Then he saw a person coming out of the house across the street. The person waved at someone in the car, then walked over to it and got in on the passenger side. The car pulled away. This time Hal did check his watch—nine-thirty, exactly.

Hal sat back down on the grass. First, he told himself that just because Ed wasn't here at nine-thirty on the dot didn't mean he wasn't coming. Besides, maybe Hal's watch was a few minutes fast—or Ed's was a few minutes slow.

Then, as the minutes ticked away, Hal tried to remember exactly what Ed had said on the phone. But that was no help.

For some reason, he recalled the first time he spoke to Ed—when Ed and Jason walked away from him to catch up with Rich. Hal consciously refused to look at his watch.

When he finally did, it was nine-fifty-six.

Hal got to his feet, gave one more look around, saw nobody, and took a deep breath. He picked up the bat and the basket of balls and walked toward the back door of the school building.

When Hal turned over the baseballs and the bat to the coach, he said, "My friend didn't show up."

"Too bad" was all the coach said.

As Hal walked back out of the school building, he gave one last look around, then turned for the walk to Ridgeway Avenue. "Yeah, too bad," he said to himself.

The two blocks from the school to the bus stop at Ridgeway Avenue seemed like a mile.

Walking along, it was not disappointment, or even anger, that Hal felt so much as it was—he swallowed, finding it difficult to even think the word—embarrassment. He had been stood up. He had not been rejected. Ed had not said no. He had said yes, and then had not shown up.

Hal almost gave a little shiver when he thought of Monday. What was he going to say when he saw Ed? "Hey, where were you?" And what would Ed say? He'd probably smile and say, "Aw, gee, man, I—"

Hal climbed into the bus and took a seat, then stared out the window. He clenched his jaw and, for the first time, felt real anger. What he would like to do, he thought, was punch Ed Patterson in the face.

The bus finally reached his stop. Hal got off, walked to his apartment house, and went in.

His mother was sitting at the table in the dining area

with stacks of file folders around her, not unusual for a Saturday morning. She used this uninterrupted quiet time to help her stay on top of her job.

Hal gave her a nod when she looked up and waited for her to say, "You're back early."

But instead she said, "The boy you were supposed to meet called soon after you left and said he couldn't make it."

"Yeah, I know," Hal said. He wished he had tried harder to keep the disappointment out of his voice. Well, what did it matter? He turned to head for his room.

"Wait a minute. It wasn't like that. He said they'd just received a phone call that his grandfather, who's been hospitalized, has taken a turn for the worse, and he had to go to Peoria with his family."

Hal felt a great sense of relief. He almost smiled. He said, "Really?"

"Uh-huh. He said he would call you when they get back, either this afternoon or evening."

Chapter 6

BY PRACTICE ON MONDAY, the memory of Hal's wait for Ed at the school and the slow trip back home seemed like ancient history.

Ed had called on Saturday evening, as promised, just as Hal and his mother were sitting down to dinner.

"Make it quick," Ellen had said, "and don't forget to ask about his grandfather."

Hal took the phone, glancing at his mother and wondering how he was supposed to make it quick and also have a conversation about Ed's grandfather's health.

"I'm sorry," Ed began. "Did you wait long?"

"No, not long," Hal said. Then he decided that something less than the complete truth was the suitable thing to say. "I figured something had happened."

"Yeah."

"How's your grandfather?" Hal asked, looking at his mother.

"He's not in good shape. He has heart trouble."

Hal wasn't sure what to say, so he said, "I'm sorry."

His mother was whirling her forefinger in a circle. Hal had seen the gesture before. He knew what it meant: Wind things up; your dinner is getting cold.

"Look, we've just started dinner, and I've got to go. Thanks for calling."

"How about tomorrow afternoon?"

"What?"

"Let's try it again tomorrow afternoon. I'll see if Jason and Rich want to come. Better to have a real pitcher—and better to have Jason there to help me chase the hits."

Hal grinned. "O-kay!" he said.

On Sunday afternoon, they couldn't borrow a basket of baseballs and a bat from the equipment room—the school was locked. But each of the boys had brought a ball, and Jason had a bat that was slimmer and lighter than Hal's. For two hours, Rich pitched and Hal swung while Ed and Jason, in short outfield positions, retrieved the balls.

Afterward, the four of them had gone to the mall for hamburgers and sodas.

Hal was taking batting practice, standing in the box, waggling a thin bat, watching Larry Milford, the left-hander on the mound, go into his windup.

Everyone on the field knew that Coach Mavis had shifted Warner Dawson to right field and put Hal at second base. Probably most of them had heard the news over the weekend. Warner and Freddie and Blaine were telling people, no doubt. Hal had told Ed, and then the word had gone out to Jason and Rich. The circle of people who knew got wider and wider.

For those who might not have heard, the evidence was there in the fielding drill when Hal took up a position at second base and Warner headed out to right field.

Nobody in the locker room or on the practice field had said anything. There were no congratulations for Hal. And there were, as far as Hal had heard, no questions or comments for Warner. Coach Mavis had made no formal announcement. He acted as if nothing had happened—Stevens at second base, Dawson in right field, that's all. As for Warner, he avoided Hal in the locker room and on the field, and Hal was glad he did.

Larry Milford brought his left arm around with a straight overhead fastball.

Hal held the bat cocked in position, watched the approaching pitch, and swung, poking a liner into short left field.

Then he laid down a bunt along the third-base line and stepped out of the box, his turn in the hitting drill finished. He walked to the side and stopped, awaiting the conclusion of the batting practice and the start of the intrasquad innings.

"Wait a minute, wait a minute." The voice was Coach

Mavis's. He was walking into the batting cage and gesturing to Hal to join him.

Surprised, Hal looked around for a moment, making sure he was the one Coach Mavis wanted. Then he walked back toward the batter's box.

"That wasn't a bunt," Don Mavis said. "That was a weak infield hit. Any decent third baseman would have thrown you out." He took Hal's bat and said, "Let me show you."

Everyone was watching. The coach had not issued a word of instruction in the first week of practice. He had watched, frowned, nodded, occasionally shook his head; but he had seldom said anything. But here he was, offering tips to the newcomer he had inserted at second base in place of the two-year starter.

Hal felt the beginnings of a blush. He did not want to be singled out by the coach. Especially not today, his first day at second base in place of Warner. But there was nothing he could do.

If the coach had any idea that it looked as if he were giving special attention to Hal, he didn't show it. He stepped into the batter's box and took a batting stance. Then he turned suddenly, facing the pitcher, as if the ball were on the way. He held the bat parallel to the ground, slightly extended from his body. His right hand slid down about halfway to the end of the bat. Then, as if the ball had arrived, he gave the bat the slightest beginning of a swing and quickly reversed its movement, drawing the bat back in and turning it at the same time toward the left, toward third base.

He looked at Hal. "A bunt that goes too far is no bunt at all," he said. "The idea is to lay the ball down gently. You want a slow roller. The slower the roll, the better chance the catcher will have to field it instead of the third baseman, and that's what you want. The catcher will have to turn to throw to first base, and that gives you an extra second to get there. So let the ball bounce off the bat—that's all, just a little bounce. And you can soften even that by pulling back the bat at the moment of contact."

Hal nodded.

"Try it," Coach Mavis said, handing the bat back to Hal. He turned to Larry on the mound. "A fastball, right down the middle," he called.

Hal stepped into the box, cocked the bat, and waited.

Larry wound up and delivered.

Hal went into the series of moves demonstrated by Coach Mavis—stepping quickly to face the pitch; sliding his right hand down the bat; poking slightly at the ball, then pulling quickly back to soften the blow.

He felt awkward performing the strange routine, and all the more so because everyone was watching. But he caught a piece of the ball with the bat and put a slow roller on the ground. The ball rolled foul.

"That's better," Coach Mavis said. "You'll need to work on it."

The intrasquad game was barely under way when, to Hal's relief, it became obvious that Coach Mavis was going to be instructing everyone. He had spent the first week of practice quietly learning the faces and names and assessing the talent on the team. Now he was teaching—not just Hal, but everyone.

At first base, he lectured Ed on the need to develop the habit of always stretching toward the throw, reaching out with his glove, to make the catch a split second earlier. The split second might mean the difference between an infield hit and an out, the coach told him, so stretching for the throw should be routine, not a special effort for close calls.

He cautioned Blaine at third base to pay close attention to the catcher's signals to the pitcher, and to position himself accordingly. For an inside pitch to a right-handed hitter, for example, Blaine should move a step closer to the foul line, expecting the hitter to pull the ball.

He gave Freddie a lesson in footwork in completing a double play: Always make the throw off the left foot.

And in right field, he instructed Warner on the fine points of keeping his body squarely behind his glove hand when gathering in a bouncer. That way, said Coach Mavis, if Warner missed the ball, his body would stop it. And that,

50

he continued, was better than having the ball bounce past him.

For Hal, the four innings of play went surprisingly well.

When he looked around the strange territory of the second baseman his first time in the field, he'd wondered what problems awaited him. But the throw to first, even from the deep second-base position, was indeed shorter than the throw from third, and he was able to make it more quickly, not needing to wind up for a long heave across the diamond. Although he had a wider area to guard, with his speed that was no problem. Hal found his confidence growing with every play.

And at bat, he took a needling from the catcher, Harry Small—"You're going to hit the ball with that twig?" he jeered—until he sent a grounder just beyond Blaine's reach at third base into left field. Yes, Hal thought as he stood on first base, a single is better than a long fly for an out.

When he came to bat in the third inning, Coach Mavis appeared at the batting cage. "Bunt it," he said. Hal nodded.

Rich, with his blazing fastball, was on the mound.

As Hal stepped into the box, Rich said something to Blaine. Obviously, Rich had heard the coach's order, and he was telling Blaine what was coming in case he hadn't heard for himself. Rich might be a friend, but he wasn't giving up any hits he could avoid, even to Hal.

Blaine crept a few steps forward and crouched, waiting.

Rich went into his windup and let go of the ball. Hal shifted into position for a bunt. Then he stepped back and let the pitch go by—outside.

With the coach's instruction confirmed, Blaine inched another step in.

Seeing Blaine so obviously positioned for a bunt, Hal glanced at Coach Mavis. The coach looked at Blaine, then back at Hal, and nodded.

Rich sent in a fastball, waist high and down the middle.

Hal swung—not a bunt, but a full swing.

The low liner was past Blaine before he had a chance to react. It would have been an easy out for a third baseman back in the proper position, but Blaine, so far forward, had no chance. He gave a little jump of surprise and a wild flailing motion with his gloved hand. But by that time the ball was bouncing on the grass in short left field, and Hal was crossing first base with a single.

As he turned to go back to the bag, Hal heard the coach's laughter from across the diamond. He looked up and Coach Mavis called out, "I think you're learning."

Chapter 7

MORE THAN ONCE IN the following days, Hal came close to telling Ed Patterson, and maybe Jason Hart and Rich Oliver, too, that his father was Ralph Stevens. After all, they were friends, on and off the field. They had helped him when he needed practice with a lighter bat. They cheered his smooth fielding at second base. They seemed to delight in his place hitting. And they had taken him into their group—on the visit to the mall, in the classroom, and in the cafeteria at lunchtime. Through them, Hal had met others, so that by the second week of practice, he was no longer an outsider.

The coolness, even resentment, of Blaine and Freddie and Warner continued, but it mattered less and less. Hal had his own friends.

Hal felt funny about keeping his secret from Ed and the others. Friends did not keep secrets from one another. Friends told one another things—everything. But whenever he took a breath and started to tell them, the words he was about to speak did not sound right in his mind. What was he supposed to do—wave everyone into silence and say, "I have an announcement to make"? No matter how he told them, would he sound like he was boasting?

Besides, how would they react to his announcement? He did not want to see the look of awe that had appeared on some of the faces around Blodgett High when the word began circulating. And he did not want to be subjected to looks that said Hal thought he was something special.

He also did not want to begin hearing—or reading about—comparisons of the father and the son on the baseball field.

It was easy to put off telling his secret. The time just never seemed right. Almost every day he told himself, Maybe today. By the end of the day he was telling himself, Well, maybe tomorrow. And Hal let the time pass.

But the longer he held the secret, the more he wondered what he was going to say in the end if they asked, "Why didn't you say so?" Why, indeed?

Hal imagined, too, the reaction of Blaine and Freddie and Warner. Warner had not spoken to Hal since being shifted to the outfield. Blaine and Freddie spoke to Hal in the infield only when necessary, and even then there was nothing friendly about their remarks. In his mind, Hal could hear them snorting that Hal Stevens thought he was better than the others because his father had been a major-league star. It was easy to imagine their references to "special treatment" by the coach for the son of Ralph Stevens. He could also hear their comparisons of him with his father.

Hal had visions of Don Mavis's finding out. "Your father was a great third baseman," Mavis would say, and Hal would flinch, knowing he was recalling Hal's mediocre throws from third base to first. "He was a powerful hitter," the coach would say, and Hal would know he was thinking of having taught him to place hit with a smaller bat because he couldn't swing a heavy one.

The comparisons with his father just wouldn't go away.

It was the second inning of the intrasquad game on Thursday. Jason Hart was on first base with a single. Warner Dawson was at bat. Rich Oliver was pitching. There were no outs.

On the mound, Rich glanced over his shoulder at Jason dancing off first base, then went into his abbreviated windup and delivered a fastball. It was low, just above the knees.

Warner waggled the big bat, took a stride forward with his left foot, and swung. He smashed the ball along the ground just to the right of the mound. Rich leaped, reached, and missed the ball.

Jason was racing toward second.

Freddie darted to his left, deep behind second base. He had his glove down and out.

Hal broke into a run to cover second base.

Freddie caught the ball and skidded to a halt just as Hal was approaching second base. He flipped the ball underhanded to Hal.

Hal took in the ball on the run as his foot hit the base. Jason was a force-out. That was one down. All that was needed now was a turn and a throw to first base for a double play.

But the ball hit Hal's glove like a stone. All the rhythm of his race for the bag, the tagging of the base, the catch, the turn, the throw—it all evaporated under the weight of the ball landing in his glove.

Hal tried to complete the play anyway. He got the ball out of his glove with his right hand, turned off balance, and sent a soaring throw to first base. The seconds lost, first in Hal's recovery from the catch and then in his sailing throw, enabled Warner to win the race. He beat the throw to first.

Hal knew instantly what had happened. Freddie had given him a "heavy" throw—a "dead ball" with no spin. It had hung in the air a second too long and then dropped lifelessly.

Sometimes a "heavy" throw was an accident—purely and simply a misplay. But sometimes it was intentional, a deliberate attempt to make a teammate look bad.

In this case, maybe Freddie had a double reason: make Hal look bad and also save his friend Warner from hitting into a double play.

Freddie grinned at Hal, and Hal was sure this had been no misplay.

Hal glared at him, and it took a moment for him to realize that the practice field was deathly quiet. There were no calls of "Nice try" or "Too bad"—the sort of thing Hal normally would have heard from Ed, Rich, and others. Obviously some of the players knew what had happened—the ones who had interpreted Freddie's grin as Hal had. Others, unsure exactly what had happened, sensed from the tension in the air that something wrong had occurred. Jason was standing beyond second base, watching in silence, a puzzled look on his face. On the mound, Rich was glowering, maybe at Freddie's acknowledgment of a bad throw, maybe at Hal's poor throw to first base.

Freddie gave a little shrug, aimed more at the others than at Hal, and said nothing.

Then the silence was shattered. "Harrison!"

It was Coach Mavis, now moving across the infield. Freddie turned toward the approaching coach and waited.

The coach walked the rest of the way to Freddie without speaking. Then he put his face in Freddie's and said—not in a shout, but loud enough to be heard—"If you ever do that again, you are on the bench."

The coach was as certain as Hal that Freddie's bad throw had been intentional.

Hal heard Freddie's voice, barely above a whisper. "Gee, I—"

Coach Mavis turned and walked back to the third-base line.

Warner, standing with a foot on first base, watched with a questioning expression. In his dash to first base, he had seen nothing of what had happened.

Jason walked past Hal. He had been concentrating on getting to second base and had not seen what had happened either. He asked, "What was that all about?"

Hal spoke softly. "I think Freddie smiled at the wrong time."

Hal was barely half-dressed in front of his locker when Coach Mavis entered the dressing room and thumbtacked a sheet of paper to the bulletin board on the wall.

"Tomorrow's starting lineup," Ed said, and walked across the room for a look.

Hal, barefooted, with his jeans on but no shirt, followed.

"You're leadoff," Ed said.

Hal looked and, yes, the first name in the batting order was *Stevens 2B*.

The role of the leadoff hitter was to get on base. It didn't matter if it was a solid hit, a scratchy single, a walk,

58

or an error. Anything would do. And Coach Mavis was betting that Hal could do it.

Hal stared at his typewritten name and reflected on what a difference a week could make. Seven days ago he was a distant second to Blaine Wilkins at third base, wielding a bat he couldn't swing. Now he was starting at second base and hitting leadoff with a thin bat that poked the ball through holes in the infield.

"You're hitting third," Hal said.

Ed laughed. "That's because I have big muscles."

When Hal came out of the locker room, Blaine Wilkins was waiting for him in the corridor. As Hal approached Blaine, Harry Small emerged, saw the two of them, and walked on without a word.

"That was a dirty trick." Blaine, half a head taller than Hal, was looking down into Hal's face.

Hal knew what he was talking about. He looked up at Blaine and said nothing for a moment. Then he snapped back, "Yes, it was, and Freddie got caught at it."

"The dirty trick was that you let Coach Mavis believe that Freddie did it on purpose."

"Didn't he?"

"No."

"How do you know?"

"Because Freddie told me he didn't."

Hal looked at Blaine. Blaine seemed to believe what he

59

was saying. "Maybe Freddie ought to tell that to Coach Mavis."

"Freddie knows it wouldn't do any good." Blaine was still scowling down at Hal. "I don't know why, but you're the coach's pet. You couldn't play third base, so he dumped Warner in right field and gave you second. Now you bungle a double play and Coach Mavis blames Freddie."

Hal glared back up into Blaine's face. Blaine and Freddie and Warner could ignore him if they wanted to. They could resent him for beating out Warner at second base. But calling him "coach's pet" touched a nerve that Blaine had no way of knowing about.

"Listen, and listen good," Hal said, "so you can go tell Warner and Freddie and anyone else who wants to hear. I did not ask to play second. It was Coach Mavis's idea. Maybe he thinks I can play second base better than Warner. If you and the others don't like the idea, too bad. And I did not bungle a double play. Freddie did it. Maybe on purpose, maybe not. But *he* bungled it. I didn't."

Hal turned and walked away from Blaine.

Chapter 8

WHEN HIS FATHER CALLED that evening, Hal was at his desk in his room trying, without much success, to concentrate on French vocabulary. Other thoughts kept shoving the French words out of his mind: the heavy throw from Freddie, Blaine's anger and Warner's resentment, the secret he was keeping from his friends and from Coach Mavis. And, on the happier side, the prospect of tomorrow's season-opening game.

He was going to be starting at second base and batting in the leadoff slot, not sitting on the bench as the second-string third baseman, watching the others on the field.

He was gaining confidence in his new position every day, and with every throw to Ed at first base he knew that second base, not third, was the place for him. And hitting with the smaller bat was not only getting better with every swing but was also feeling more comfortable.

So Hal should be smiling at the way his world at Cannon City High was shaping up, right? Sure, but then why was he having trouble keeping his mind and eyes on the list of words in front of him?

Hal stopped trying to concentrate on the vocabulary when the phone rang. He turned his head toward the door and waited while his mother answered the telephone. Maybe it was Freddie Harrison calling to apologize for the heavy throw. Maybe it was Blaine wanting to make some peace. Maybe Ed wanted to talk about the upcoming game.

Then, from the way his mother talked, he knew it was his father calling. She spoke in a different tone when he was on the other end of the line. She was always friendly, courteous—but a little distant, which was not her usual manner. She always told his father that she was well, that everything was going along just fine, and then she asked about him. Also, she always asked about Gloria, his father's second wife. This done, she always handed the telephone to Hal with the words, "It's your father." The routine occurred every two or three weeks, usually on a Sunday evening.

Hal came out of his room, gave his mother a little nod, and took the phone.

As Ellen Stevens disappeared around the corner into her bedroom, Hal sat down at the desk with the telephone. This was also part of the routine. His mother left him alone to speak with his father.

Hal cleared his throat and took a deep breath. He had a

62

feeling of dread that he couldn't explain. He had not spoken with his father since the baseball season started. Ralph Stevens was going to ask about his health, his schoolwork, and, yes, baseball. What was he going to think about Hal's playing second base? Sure, he would be pleased that Hal was in the starting lineup. But why second base? Why not third? Was Ralph Stevens going to be disappointed that the son couldn't make it at the father's position?

Hal was frowning as he began to speak.

The talk quickly turned to baseball.

"I'm playing second base," Hal said without preamble.

"Second base?"

Hal explained that the coach—"the coach," not "Coach Don Mavis"—had concluded that he didn't have a strong enough right arm to play third but should do well at second base because of the shorter throw to first.

"Really?"

"Yeah," Hal said. He wanted to add that surely his father knew that his son did not have his own powerful physique. But how would that sound?

"What do you think about it?" Ralph asked.

"It seems to be working out."

"Second base, huh?" To Hal, his father's questioning tone seemed to be implying that second base was for sissies, third base for men. But maybe it was his imagination. "I always thought you would be a third baseman," his father added, "like your old man." He gave a small laugh.

Hal let his father's comment pass without offering any further explanation. Instead, he said, "I'm batting leadoff." He went on to tell about using a lighter bat and working on place hitting and bunting on the coach's advice—again, "the coach," not "Coach Don Mavis."

"Hmm, your coach seems to have lots of ideas for you."

"Uh-huh, well, some."

Hal wondered why he didn't want to tell his father that "the coach" was Don Mavis. Then he knew why. Unlike Don Mavis, Ralph Stevens had nothing shy or boyish in his manner. His father was the kind to call Don Mavis and ask, "How's my kid doing?" Or, worse yet, "Who says my boy can't play third base?" Hal did not want either of those things to happen.

"I'd sure like to see you play sometime."

Hal said, "Yeah, but Cannon City is a long way from New York."

"Maybe I can work it out one of these days."

"Yeah, that'd be great."

Ralph Stevens then asked the usual questions about school, and Hal gave the usual answers: Everything was going fine, no problems. It took a lot of reading to catch up in American history and English literature, but he was making it okay.

Then Hal asked his father the obligatory question: "How's Gloria?"

Hal's mother insisted on the question. "She's your father's wife," Ellen had said, apparently thinking that that explained everything. To Hal, it didn't matter. Gloria had been nice enough whenever he had been around her, but he hardly knew her.

"Gloria's fine, and sends her love." His father always said that.

Hal said good-bye, hung up the telephone slowly, and remained seated at the desk, recalling his father's lukewarm response to his announcement about playing second base. Was Ralph Stevens disappointed that his son wasn't following in his footsteps as a third baseman? Hal didn't know. But he did know his feet weren't big enough to fill his father's baseball shoes. And now his father knew it, too.

Chapter 9

THE BELL RANG, ENDING the class, and Hal gathered up his books and got to his feet with the other students. American history was the last class before lunch. He glanced across at Ed and Jason. The three of them usually dropped off their books in their lockers and headed for the cafeteria together.

Hal hadn't seen Blaine—or Freddie or Warner, for that matter—during the morning. The three of them were seniors, and Hal had no classes with them. Luck had kept him from meeting them in the halls. He hoped the luck would hold through the lunch hour.

He moved with the stream of students toward the door.

"Mr. Stevens—a moment?"

As always, Hal was a little startled at being addressed as Mr. Stevens. He turned and saw Mr. Henderson, the American history teacher, standing behind his desk at the front of the room, smiling and beckoning to him.

With a glance toward Ed and Jason, Hal stepped out of the line of students and walked toward the teacher's desk.

It couldn't be a classwork problem. American history gave Hal less trouble than any of the other subjects he was still catching up on.

"Yes, sir?" Hal said, stepping in front of Mr. Henderson's desk.

"I didn't know your father was Ralph Stevens," Mr. Henderson said.

Hal felt his heart skip a beat. Without thinking, he looked around. Ed gave him a questioning glance from just outside the door, out of earshot, and then disappeared. Nobody next to him was paying attention. The closest students were three girls chatting among themselves.

"Yes," Hal said.

Mr. Henderson beamed at Hal. "I've been a Cardinals fan since I was a boy."

"Oh?" He wondered where his teacher had found out about his father.

Mr. Henderson immediately cleared up the puzzle for Hal. "My wife works in personnel at Walters Medical, and she knows your mother."

Hal nodded imperceptibly. So the word was beginning to get around the way he figured it would—from his mother at her office. And it was bound to spread. Perhaps Mr. Henderson had already told others.

"So," Mr. Henderson said, still smiling, "you certainly come by your baseball skills honestly."

There it is, Hal thought—a comparison with his father.

For a moment he wondered how the American history teacher knew that he was on the baseball team—the team hadn't yet played its first game. Maybe his mother had mentioned it in discussing his father.

Mr. Henderson continued without giving Hal a chance to speak. "The first game is this afternoon, isn't it?"

Hal wanted to get away before the teacher turned the conversation back to his father, perhaps saying something that the last of the departing students could hear. "Yes," he said, "we're playing the Pritchard Buccaneers."

Mr. Henderson nodded his head a couple of times to signal the end of the conversation. "Good luck," he said.

"Thanks."

Hal came out of the classroom looking for his friends in the hall. He knew that he had to tell them about Ralph Stevens right away, before they heard from someone else—from a casual acquaintance who knew more about their friend Hal Stevens than they did, or, worse yet, Blaine or Warner or Freddie.

He'd been telling himself it was no big deal and had then let the time drag on without saying anything.

Well, now it was just that—a big deal.

Ed and Jason were nowhere to be seen. They must have gone on to the cafeteria without him, not knowing how long he might be tied up with Mr. Henderson. Hal made a quick stop at his locker, dropped off his books, and headed for the cafeteria.

Jason was already through the line, seated as usual at a table with his girlfriend. Ed and Rich were walking past the last of the food and coming out of the line. Hal picked up a tray and stepped into line.

Rich looked back at him and gestured at a table, and Hal nodded.

Moving along in front of the steam trays, Hal could barely bring the food into focus. He was framing what he was going to say when he sat down with Ed and Rich.

"Have you ever heard of Ralph Stevens?" Hal asked.

It was a dumb way to begin. Everyone in the world had heard of Ralph Stevens, twice the National League batting champion, three times a winner of the Golden Glove award for excellent fielding. But Hal could think of nothing better.

Ed said, "The ballplayer? Sure, why?"

Rich said, in a sort of slow, questioning way, "Stevens?"

Hal looked at him. Rich was picking up the thread.

Then Ed, catching the question in Rich's voice, turned to Hal and asked, "Are you related to him?"

"He's my father."

Rich frowned and said, "No kidding." Then he watched Hal and said nothing else.

"Really?" Ed said, and then asked the question that Rich had left unspoken: "Why the big secret? Why didn't you say so?"

"Well," Hal said, taking a breath, "that's what I want to talk to you about."

Rich waited without speaking.

Ed, grinning, looked from Hal to Rich and said, "If my father was one of the best third baseman who ever played, I think I'd be wearing a sign around my neck."

Hal gave a little smile and said, "Maybe not."

By the time Hal finished, the cafeteria had almost emptied. Ed, to Hal's left, and Rich, sitting across from him, had listened without interruption. When he told them about his experiences at Blodgett High that led to his vow to keep his secret as long as possible after moving to Cannon City, they seemed to understand. When he traced the events at Cannon City High that made his secret all the more important to keep—Don Mavis, a contemporary and an acquaintance of Ralph Stevens's, signing on as baseball coach; Hal wanting to succeed or fail on his own without the record of a famous father getting mixed up in the scene—they nodded, yes, maybe.

But when he talked about replacing Warner at second base, and the possible charge of favoritism—and his fear that Coach Mavis might even put Warner back at second just to prove that there was no favoritism—they nodded, but with both of them it seemed more a gesture of understanding than one of agreement. Ed was frowning. Rich shook his head slightly, almost in disagreement.

Hal leaned back. "Mr. Henderson knows; he told me so this morning. His wife works at Walters Medical with my mother, so I guess the word is going to get around. I wanted you guys to hear it from me." He paused. "I hope you'll keep it to yourselves—except for Jason—as long as possible."

Ed and Rich spoke together, both saying, "I think—" and then both stopping to let the other proceed.

Hal looked at Rich.

"I think you're mistaken about Coach Mavis. He's not going to play favorites. And he's not going to let anyone accuse him of it. Blaine, Warner, Freddie—the others don't matter."

Hal said, "Maybe." He turned to Ed.

"The word's as good as out if Mr. Henderson knows," Ed said with a shrug. "He loves to find out things and tell people—be the first to know."

"I wondered about explaining things to him and

asking him not to broadcast it," Hal told his friends.

Ed shook his head. "Forget it. All you'd get is a lecture about your head being screwed on wrong."

"Ed's right," Rich added.

Hal took a breath and looked at his watch. "The bell's about to ring."

Chapter 10

HAL AND JASON HURRIED out of their French class at the end of the day and headed for the locker room.

"I'll bet Rich is going nuts," Jason said. "He always gets uptight when he's going to pitch."

Hal smiled and said, "Oh?"

"How about you?"

"Me? I'm okay. Looking forward to it."

They turned the corner at the bottom of the stairs and walked toward the dressing room.

Right now, Hal's mind was more on what was beyond the locker-room door than what awaited him on the playing field. If Mr. Henderson's news had reached Warner Dawson's ears—or Blaine's or Freddie's—he might be starting his first game at second base with "coach's pet" ringing in his ears and his teammates sizing up the shortcomings of Ralph Stevens's son.

But when Hal and Jason pushed through the door and headed for their lockers, Warner, Blaine, and Freddie said nothing—nothing at all. And there was nothing more than the usual nods and murmurings of greetings from the other players.

Normal, thought Hal with a sigh of relief.

Coach Mavis was making the rounds of the players with his easygoing style and friendly smile. "Ready, Hal?" the coach asked.

Nothing new there, either.

"Right, ready," Hal said.

Ed's eyes showed his excitement at the prospect of the first game. "Here we go," he announced with a grin.

Hal couldn't help smiling back at his friend.

Rich was not grinning. Jason's prediction had been correct. The starting pitcher was a picture of intensity. He nodded curtly to Hal.

Then Hal put all his thoughts of "coach's pet" out of his mind and began changing into his uniform.

The first hitter for the Pritchard High Buccaneers sent a grounder to Hal's left. Hal moved over, scooped up the ball, and easily threw out the runner.

Hal knew that for a lot of players, in any sport, their first play was important. A sort of nervousness hung on until they succeeded in catching a baseball without error, or plunging into the line without fumbling the football, or scoring the first shot in a basketball game. But Hal never felt this nervousness about baseball. He eagerly—not nervously—awaited the first play, and all those that followed. He wished that every batter would hit the ball to him.

Rich struck out the next batter and got the third on a pop fly to Blaine.

Hal ran to the bench, dropped his glove, picked up his bat, and walked toward the plate to lead off for the Gunners. Standing back, he took a couple of warm-up swings while the Pritchard High pitcher threw his three warm-up pitches. Then he stepped into the batter's box, cocked his bat, stared at the pitcher, and waited.

The first pitch, a fastball, whistled by, a shade high, and the umpire called ball one.

Hal heard Ed's voice from the bench. "Let's go, Hal!"

The second pitch came in waist high. Hal watched the ball approaching and tightened his grip on the bat. He swung and connected. The ball came off the bat in a low liner between the third baseman and the shortstop, hitting the ground on the edge of the outfield grass. By the time the left fielder took in the ball on the second bounce, Hal had crossed first base.

Jason, the Gunners' center fielder, batting second, fouled out to the third baseman.

Ed strode to the plate and promptly smashed the first pitch for a scorching line drive—straight into the Pritchard High shortstop's glove.

Hal, off and running with the crack of the bat, slammed on the brakes, whirled, and dived back to first base, barely beating the shortstop's throw for a double play.

He stood on the base, dusting himself off, while Warner stepped into the batter's box. Then, as Warner positioned himself and fixed a hard stare on the pitcher, Hal danced a few steps off the base.

Warner was a menacing sight at the plate—tall, with heavily muscled arms. He peered over his thick shoulder at the pitcher and waggled the heavy bat easily, his large hands as close to the end as possible, in order to increase the arc of his swing and add power.

Clearly, Warner Dawson's big bat would play an important role if the Gunners were going to have a good season and a good showing in the state tournament.

Hal called out, "Hey! Hey! Let's go!" before he remembered that the batter was a teammate who never spoke to him.

Warner took two pitches, the first outside for a ball, the second for a called strike. Then he swung at the third pitch and missed, for strike two.

The fourth pitch was a fastball coming in high. Warner twitched the bat a little, stepped out with his left foot, and swung with everything he had.

With two outs and two strikes on Warner, there was no risk in his running, so Hal broke into a sprint when he saw Warner starting to bring the bat around. He was more than halfway to second base when he heard the sharp crack of the bat on the ball. Warner had connected.

Hal rounded second base and made the turn for third. Out of the corner of his eye he saw the Pritchard High left fielder looking up at the ball with a shrug. And then Hal saw the ball drop beyond the low chain-link fence at the edge of the outfield for a home run. He slowed to a jog, touched third base, and trotted home.

After he crossed home plate, he turned and waited.

Warner, making the turn at third base, was grinning.

As Warner crossed home plate, Hal extended his right hand. Warner, looking past Hal rather than at him, veered toward the bench, heading past the outstretched hand. Then, still not looking at Hal, Warner reached out at the last second and slapped hands.

Hal frowned and jogged toward the bench behind Warner and into the crowd of cheering players coming out to greet him.

Blaine Wilkins grounded out to second base to end the inning.

Rich Oliver, with his whiplike right arm, put the Buccaneers down in order in the first three innings, striking out four. Then he yielded a double with one out in the fourth inning. But that threat evaporated when Hal leaped desperately to his right to catch a line drive and then, while falling, pitched underhand to Freddie Harrison at second base to catch the runner trying to return.

The Gunners fared no better on the attack. Hal, in his second trip to the plate, drew a walk and died on first base. And in his third at bat, he grounded out to the shortstop. Warner struck out and flied out to center field in his next two times at bat. The Gunners weren't able to get anyone past second. Obviously, the Pritchard High pitcher had settled down after feeding the fatal fastball to Warner in the first inning.

The score stood at 2–0 through the end of the sixth inning.

In the top of the seventh, Rich walked the first batter. The second hitter sent a grounder to Hal's left—the perfect setup for an easy double play. Hal moved over, scooped up the ball in his glove hand, took it out with his right hand as he turned, and threw to Freddie at second base. Freddie tagged the base and threw to first for the double play.

Hal felt a tingle of excitement at being part—the starting point, actually—of a perfectly executed double play. As a third baseman, he seldom had been part of a double play. Now in his first game as a second baseman, he had started one, and it felt good.

Walking off the mound, Rich turned and actually smiled.

Hal took off his glove and ran toward the bench.

"You're up," somebody said.

Startled, Hal looked up. Yes, he was the batter. He

dropped off his glove, found his bat, and ran to the plate.

The pitcher forced a fastball past him for a called strike. Then came a change of pace—a slow floater, maybe the Pritchard High pitcher's idea of a knuckleball. Whatever it was, it was a mistake. The ball came drifting in, a sitting duck. A slugger like Warner would have wound up and knocked it into the next county. Hal, without thinking, turned to face the ball, slid his right hand down the bat a few inches, and laid down a bunt. The soft pitch barely bounced off the bat. The ball hit the ground on the third-base side and rolled slowly in a wobbling route.

Hal dropped the bat and sprinted for first base. He sensed rather than saw the catcher peeling off his mask and scrambling after the ball. That was good. As Coach Mavis had said, the catcher would have to turn to make the throw.

Hal's foot hit the first-base bag, and a second later he heard the thump of the ball in the first baseman's mitt. He was safe.

Jason singled to left field, advancing Hal to second.

Ed worked the count to three balls and two strikes, then pounded out a long fly that backed the right fielder almost to the fence. At first, Hal thought Ed had hit a home run. But he hung close to his base, in case the towering fly fell short of the fence. After the right fielder caught the ball, Hal returned and tagged up.

Then the right fielder made an assumption—nobody

was going to try to advance after a routine fly to right field—and committed the sin of laziness. In leisurely fashion, he took the ball out of his glove, cocked his arm for a soft throw to the second baseman, and lofted the ball into the air.

Hal suddenly broke into a sprint for third base. He was two-thirds of the way there before the easy throw took a bounce and the frantic second baseman got his hands on the ball. As the second baseman was turning for his throw to third, Hal leaped into a headfirst slide and got his hands on the bag. A wide throw pulled the third baseman away from the bag to make the catch.

Warner, next up, delivered the needed fly to the outfield. Hal held close to third until the left fielder caught the ball. Then he tagged the base and ran home, scoring standing up.

The game ended two innings later with the score still 3–0.

By the time of the final out—a high fly to Warner in right field—the sun was low and casting long shadows, and the slight breeze of the later afternoon had turned chilly.

Hal was sorry to see the finish of the game. He could not remember having had so much fun on a baseball field—and for Hal Stevens, that was saying something.

He had fielded flawlessly in his new position. Gone was the nagging worry about the long throw across the diamond from third base to first. He made his throw easily now, and with greater accuracy and a newfound confidence.

At the plate, Hal had gotten two hits and scored two of his team's runs. With the lighter bat he found himself relying on his eyes, shoulders, arms, hands—and brain—to hit the ball, rather than the prayers needed with the big bat. He hadn't struck out once—a regular occurrence when he was swinging the bludgeon.

Hal felt himself on the brink of a whole new world of baseball.

Then, as he began jogging toward the school building, he realized something. Suddenly, without any warning at all, it hit him: He was no longer in his father's shadow.

Today, during the fierce competition of a real game, he saw—clearly, for the first time—that the shadow of his father was gone. He was Hal Stevens, a second baseman, whereas his father had been a third baseman. He was now a place hitter and a bunter whereas his father had been a slugger.

Father and son were two different people!

Nobody would be able to make comparisons now, because there was nothing to compare.

Hal felt like shouting out, "I'm me, Dad, not you," but instead he just smiled to himself and followed Harry Small through the door and into the hallway leading to the locker room.

Chapter 11

PRACTICE SESSIONS, GAMES, AND classroom work rolled along the next two weeks, all of them getting better with each passing day.

On the practice field, Hal worked on his bunting and place hitting. More and more, the bunts would drop where he wanted them and roll as slowly as he liked. His place hitting included instruction in hitting to the opposite field—learning to curb his natural tendency as a right-handed batter to pull the ball toward left field and instead poke it toward right field. To be able to hit behind a runner sprinting from first to second was a valuable skill.

In the next three games, all of them victories for the Gunners, Hal had four hits—all of them singles—and three walks in thirteen trips.

At the second-base position, he speared line drives, caught pop-ups, scooped up grounders, and took in bouncers, all with only one error—a horrifying bobble that left him paralyzed with embarrassment for a moment.

The Barber High Leopards had a runner on first with no outs when the batter sent a bouncer to Hal's left. It was the perfect setup for a double play. Hal moved over and made the easy catch. He took the ball out of the glove, turned to pitch it to Freddie at second base, and...dropped it. Hal felt his face flush. He couldn't move; this was impossible. Then he scrambled after the ball. But by that time the runners were safe at second and first.

He took a breath and positioned himself for the next play. He nodded when Ed called out, "It's okay," shrugged at Rich, who was glaring at him from the mound. He avoided looking at Freddie or at Coach Mavis.

Then he told himself, It was Hal Stevens at second base who fumbled, not the son of Ralph Stevens at third.

It was odd, but the fumble was reassuring.

Even more reassuring was the telephone call from Don Mavis that evening. "I just wanted you to know that I booted a double play exactly the same way in the first World Series game I played in," he said.

So it was not just hitting and fielding but also, in a weird way, fumbling that contributed to Hal's happier view of the world as the days passed.

There were no more "heavy" throws by Freddie either in practice sessions or in games. If the first one had been intentional, Freddie obviously had taken Coach Mavis's threat to heart and decided against any repeats. If it was accidental, as Blaine insisted, Freddie was avoiding another accident. Either way, there was no repetition of the misplay.

As a matter of fact, in both practice sessions and games, Freddie seemed to be getting friendlier in their play around second base. He would tell Hal "Nice play" on occasion. Sometimes he gave just a nod and a little wave—but that was almost the same as a spoken compliment.

Even Blaine came through with a high five or a call of "Nice running" when Hal scored.

But in the locker room, before and after practice sessions and games, Blaine, Freddie, and Warner hung out together, sometimes joking with others—although never with Hal. And Hal never made a move to break through the wall they had placed around themselves.

On the field, though, Hal cheered. When Blaine made a nice stop at third base, recovered quickly, and then rifled the ball across the infield for the out, Hal sang out, "Way to go!" He did the same with Freddie—"Beautiful! Beautiful!"

Ed, from his vantage point at first base, watched with a frown when Blaine and Freddie seemed to be trying to freeze out Hal and smiled when Hal shouted out a word of praise for them.

"You're cheering for guys who hardly speak to you," Ed said as they walked in the hallway between classes one day. Then he laughed. "But, then, I guess they can't argue with you when you're telling them how great they are."

Hal agreed, but he said nothing.

With Warner, there was no crack in the ice. He trooped sullenly to and from his position in right field each inning in the games. Once, after a spectacular running catch near the foul line in deep right field, Hal had called out, "Great catch!" Warner had not acknowledged the compliment with so much as a glance as he heaved the ball to Hal in the infield. In practice, Warner shagged flies and fielded bouncers with a great show of indifference. It was as if nothing that happened in right field mattered to him.

At the plate, though, Warner was anything but indifferent. He always went up to bat with teeth clenched in determination, as if he could prove with his hitting that Coach Mavis had been wrong in sending him to right field. With his powerful shoulders and arms, plus perfect rhythm in his swing, he smashed towering flies and scorching line drives all over the outfield. He hit four home runs and two doubles in the Gunners' first four games.

Hal had quit reaching for Warner's hand for a slap of congratulations after that embarrassing moment in the first game. But he had to agree with Coach Mavis that the Gunners needed Warner's bat in the lineup if they were going to have a successful season.

Hal gave up even the semblance of making friends

with Warner after two small episodes—small, maybe, in the eyes of an uninterested onlooker, but not small at all to Hal.

In the cafeteria line, Hal found himself behind Warner. The two of them ignored each other. Then the boy in front of Warner—a stranger to Hal—turned to Warner. "I hear that you're playing in right field," he said. "I thought you always played second base."

It was a bad thing for Warner to hear. But even worse for him to hear it in Hal's presence.

Hal did not catch Warner's mumbled reply.

Then during batting practice that afternoon, Coach Mavis stepped in to make a correction in Hal's swing. From long habit, Hal still sometimes swung from the heels. "Always, always," the coach said, "pick your spot, aim for it, and hit the ball into it—like this." He demonstrated, and Hal nodded.

From behind him, Hal heard Warner's voice, in a matter-of-fact conversational tone: "Coach's pet."

Hal was sure that Coach Mavis heard Warner. But the coach simply handed the bat back to Hal and said, "Try it again."

Without looking around, Hal took the bat and stepped back into the box. He shrugged and said nothing. If Coach Mavis wanted to let the remark slide by, he would do the same.

After all, Hal figured, everything was going well. He had mastered the change to second base, his batting average was respectable, and, as he had hoped, baseball had brought him some friends at the new school.

Plus, as the days passed, he worried less and less about Mr. Henderson's discovery spreading. The teacher had made no further mention to Hal of his father's fame and, as far as he could tell, had not mentioned it to anyone else.

Hal was coming to the conclusion that Cannon City High wasn't so bad after all.

It was Thursday, the day before the undefeated Gunners would board the team bus for the forty-mile ride to Franklinville to play the undefeated Falcons—the Gunners' first major test of the young season. Franklinville High, about the same size as Cannon City High, was a perennial baseball power in western Illinois. This year, the Falcons were loaded with sluggers, averaging almost nine runs a game.

When the players came out of the locker room for the start of practice, the weather was windy and cloudy, threatening rain. Hal walked onto the field looking at the sky. Gray clouds were racing by.

"No rain," Don Mavis said behind him. "The weatherman promised."

Hal turned. Coach Mavis was smiling. Hal returned the

grin and saw Warner beyond the coach, taking in the exchange. Hal could almost hear Warner repeating, "Coach's pet," and the smile faded from his face.

Following the stretching session and a jog to the outfield fence and back, the players moved into their fielding drills.

For Hal in the infield, the wind was no problem. He was gobbling up grounders, fielding bouncers, and taking the occasional line drive—unaffected by the wind. Even pop flies, although they sometimes wavered a little, were not a great problem for the infielders.

The outfield was another matter. The long, towering flies did crazy things when hit by a gust of wind. The ball, slowed in flight, dropped far in front of the fielder. Or, carried along by a burst of wind, it sailed over the outfielder. Hal heard Jason yelp a couple of times and turned to see him making a desperate last-second lunge for a ball blown off course.

When Blaine was fielding a grounder at third base, and Hal was out of the play, he watched a high fly soar toward right field. He turned, following the path of the ball. Warner moved up, face turned to the sky. He had his glove up. Then, without warning, the falling ball veered to Warner's right. Not much, but enough. Warner leaped awkwardly, and almost fell. His glove missed the ball, and it hit him on the shoulder.

Then Hal watched as Warner righted himself, seemed

to say something, and then took off his glove and threw it on the ground. He stared at the glove a moment, then picked it up and began walking off the field.

Coach Mavis appeared as if by magic, walking across the foul line toward Warner.

"I know it's frustrating," Hal heard Coach Mavis call out, "but we might find ourselves getting a little wind during a game, and the practice is useful."

Warner glared at Don Mavis, then turned and walked back to his position.

"Stevens! You want to try to catch one?"

Hal turned. Harry Small, who was doing the hitting for the infielders, was waving the bat at him.

Hal grinned sheepishly and nodded.

Harry sent a bouncer to Hal's right. Hal took two steps, brought in the ball at the top of the bounce, and threw to Ed at first base.

Past Ed, Hal saw a man standing next to the bleachers. He was wearing a blue blazer, gray slacks, and a shirt open at the neck, and he was staring directly at him.

It was Ralph Stevens.

Chapter 12

HAL GAVE A LITTLE wave, and his father waved back. Then Hal turned his gaze back to Harry, who was tossing the ball in the air and hitting a grounder toward Freddie.

Out of the corner of his eye he saw—and his heart seemed to come up in his throat—Don Mavis walking toward his father. And now his father walking toward Don Mavis.

Freddie caught the bouncer and threw the ball across to Ed at first base.

In his position at second base, Hal watched Ed catch the ball, then looked at the two men beyond first base.

They came together and shook hands for what seemed like forever. Then Ralph Stevens put his left hand over the clasped right hands. It looked like two old friends meeting after a long absence.

Hal turned back to the plate and watched the blurry picture of Harry batting the ball to Blaine, and then Blaine scooping the ball out of the dirt and firing it across the diamond to Ed. The scene was like something out of a dream, all mixed up with the thoughts racing through his mind. Don Mavis was going to ask Hal, "Why didn't you tell me?" And he was going to say...yes, what was he going to say? He should have told Coach Mavis back when he told Ed, Rich, and Jason. He should have told everyone. It was crazy to think that he could keep the secret forever. And now, well, keeping the secret at all seemed crazy. He could never explain to his father that people compared their skills as third basemen, that guys on the team stared at him in awe, and that—most of all—he wanted to be Hal Stevens instead of the son of Ralph Stevens.

The next hit was coming to him. He crouched in position and gave Harry every bit of concentration he could muster. The ball coming off the bat looked the size of an aspirin. How could he catch a bouncing aspirin?

Hal took a step forward, then one to the left, and gloved the ball easily. He took the ball in his right hand and tossed it to Ed.

Ed caught the throw and came off the base, sending a slow bouncer in Harry's direction. "Who's that?" he asked Hal.

The question at first surprised Hal. But then he realized that Ed probably had seen him wave, and his father wave in return.

"My father," Hal said.

Ed backed up to the base to take a throw from Blaine.

Beyond Ed, Don Mavis and Ralph Stevens were standing side by side. Hal's father was saying something, and Don Mavis was smiling as he listened.

Then Coach Mavis took a couple of steps forward, gave a great swooping motion with his right arm, and called out, "Okay, okay. C'mon in and let's hit a few. Rich Oliver throwing."

Hal gave a tentative glance in the direction of the bleachers, and Coach Mavis called, "Hal," gesturing for him to join them.

Hal began walking toward the two men.

Warner, running in from right field, crossed in front of Hal. He did not look at Hal but did glance at Coach Mavis and the stranger.

"Yeah, yeah," Hal said to himself, watching Warner, "coach's pet."

Ralph Stevens greeted him with an outstretched arm for a handshake. "You're looking good," he said.

"You too."

"We've got a good second baseman," Coach Mavis said.

Hal waited for him to say, "You never told me...." But instead the coach said to Hal, "Don't miss your turn at bat." Then he turned back to Hal's father. "Come on over to the bench. The boys will want to meet you."

"Sure," his father said easily, used to being the one everyone wanted to meet, "in a minute."

Don Mavis walked away and Hal saw the players gawking at him. By now Ed had surely answered their questions. Yes, Ralph Stevens, the third baseman, was Hal's father.

His father was talking to him. "I hope I didn't surprise you too much," he said. "I was in Chicago for a couple of meetings at an airport hotel and one of them was canceled, leaving me with most of the day free. It was a short flight to Cannon City, so here I am."

"That's good." Hal didn't know what else to say.

"Actually, the surprise was mine, seeing Don Mavis out there on the field. You didn't tell me he was your coach."

"I guess not."

Ralph Stevens began walking toward the bench, and Hal walked with him.

"I called Ellen from the airport in Chicago." He always called her "Ellen" instead of "your mother," which Hal thought was odd. His mother always referred to him as "your father," not "Ralph." "I wanted to be sure you were here, and not off at an away game or something."

"We've got a game trip tomorrow."

"You're starting at second base?"

"Yes."

"Very good."

Hal gave his father a questioning glance but said nothing. He had sounded cool to the idea of Hal's playing second base when they spoke on the telephone. But now he seemed genuinely pleased, maybe even proud, that his son was the starting second baseman.

They reached the bench and Ralph Stevens began introducing himself to everyone. The practice came to a halt. Rich walked over from the mound. Freddie left the batter's box. At one point, Hal's father stuck out his hand to Warner Dawson and said, "I'm Ralph Stevens." Warner shook hands with him.

Hal watched from the side. His father was assuming that everyone knew who he was. And he was right—everyone did. Nobody was asking, "Who did he say he was?" The questioning looks were directed at Hal: If Ralph Stevens is your father, why didn't you say so? But nobody said anything to him.

Coach Mavis allowed the handshaking to go on another couple of minutes, then called out, "Okay! The social period is over. We've got work to do."

Hal's father moved over and took a seat on the bench.

With Rich back on the mound and Freddie back in the batter's box, Hal walked across to the rack and selected his bat. He was standing next to Blaine when Warner, ignoring Hal, leaned in and said, "Well, that explains everything, doesn't it?"

Ralph Stevens watched the practice from the bench, mostly with Don Mavis seated next to him. During the

94

three game-condition innings, Hal fielded two grounders and a pop fly and singled once in two trips to the plate.

After practice, his father waited, chatting with Coach Mavis and some of the players while Hal showered and dressed. Then the two of them headed for dinner at the Leland House. "Ellen's recommendation," his father said.

Hal knew his mother liked the Leland House, where she occasionally ate lunch and sometimes had business dinners, but he had never eaten there before. After one look at the chandeliers and the paneled walls, the carpets, and the tuxedoed waiters, he wished he had suggested Pizza World. But it was too late now, and his father seemed pleased with the looks of the Leland House.

The formal-looking waiter was taking away the salad plates when his father said it. "Don Mavis says you never mentioned that I was your father." There was no accusatory tone. He said the words matter-of-factly, as if he were commenting on the weather.

Hal was ready for the statement, even waiting for it.

For sure, Don Mavis would have mentioned it as soon as he recognized the visitor, and Ralph Stevens would have said something like, "That's my son, Hal." Then Coach Mavis would have said something like, "Really, I didn't know." It was natural that Coach Mavis would comment on it.

"No, I didn't," Hal said slowly. "I never mentioned it. It just never seemed the right time."

Strangely, his father didn't seem to mind. At least, he was smiling at Hal.

"It was no big deal either way, here at Cannon City High," Hal added. "I mean, it had nothing to do with how well I played ball."

"Sure. I understand."

Hal wasn't sure that his father really did, but he said nothing.

"Don did know, of course."

Hal gave his father a startled look. "He did?"

"Sure. He checked the files on every one of his players. I suppose any coach would do the same. A coach wants to know who the players are. And right there in your file was my name and address. He knew vaguely that I was in advertising in New York—same as I knew vaguely that he was farming in western Illinois—and he didn't have any trouble putting two and two together."

"He never—"

"Never said anything. No. He figured that you were keeping it to yourself because you didn't want to give the impression you were seeking special treatment, because your father and your coach knew each other from way back. And that if you wanted it that way, he was willing to go along."

Hal nodded slowly. He should have known that that was why Don Mavis wasn't surprised at the sight of Ralph Stevens on the practice field. That was why he didn't ask

Hal the feared question: "Why didn't you tell me?"

"Yeah, something like that," Hal said.

After a moment, his father said, "Don tells me that you've made the switch from third to second without any problems."

"Did he tell you about my fumble?"

Ralph Stevens laughed. "Yes," he said, and then added, "We all fumble sometimes. The important thing is not to make a habit of it."

Hal said, "I like second base." Then he looked at his father and waited for a reaction.

"Good. It looks like the position for you. Don thinks so, and he knows what he's doing."

Hal waited. Was that all? Wasn't his father going to say or even hint, as he'd seemed to do on the telephone, that he was disappointed his son wasn't playing third base?

When his father didn't speak, Hal decided to open the subject himself. He wanted to clear the air. "You didn't sound exactly enthusiastic about it when I told you on the phone a couple of weeks ago."

"I was surprised, that's all. I've always thought of you as a third baseman"—Ralph paused, smiled, and interjected, "in the father's footsteps, you know"—and then continued, "and you have always played third base. So I was surprised. But after thinking about it—and after talking with Don today—I'm sure it's a good move for you."

Then Ralph Stevens told about a friend, his teammate

at second base with the Cardinals, who played third base in college and never would have made the grade in the major leagues if he hadn't shifted positions.

Hal recognized the second baseman's name, even remembered meeting him during the one spring training he had attended with his parents before their divorce. That was a long time ago, back when the three of them were a family, but most of the events of those days were etched deeply in Hal's memory.

Hal shrugged off the flashback. "Really? I didn't know he had been a third baseman."

"He was an average third baseman—but a great second baseman. I used to envy him. He had the speed to range all over the field. I didn't have his kind of speed and never could have played second base like he did. I was better at third base than I ever would have been at second."

Hal watched his father. He'd never heard him express envy of another player's abilities, at third base or any other position. But here he was, saying that an average third baseman had turned into a standout second baseman, one whom Ralph Stevens could not match.

"Maybe it'll be the same way for you," his father said with a smile. "Don Mavis says you've got the speed for it." He paused, then added, "It's all a matter of maximizing your strong points and minimizing your weak ones. We've all got some of both."

* * *

It was eight o'clock when Hal's father dropped him off at the apartment and headed back to the airport to turn in the rental car and catch the last commuter flight to Chicago.

Hal waved to the car pulling away from the curb, and his father beeped the horn lightly and then was gone.

Hal stood a moment in the darkness. The wind had blown itself away, and the spring evening was quiet and still. Already, he missed his father. He had liked having Ralph watch him hitting and fielding. He'd enjoyed the dinner conversation. And he was immensely relieved to know that his father did not consider him a failure because he could not follow in his footsteps as a third baseman.

Walking down the short sidewalk to the door, he almost smiled at the thought that Don Mavis had known all along that he was the son of Ralph Stevens. All that worry and fret—for no good reason.

And now the secret was known by all the players—not just Ed and Rich and Jason, but all the others, including Warner, Blaine, and Freddie. Hal wondered what they were thinking.

Chapter 13

"WARNER'S NOT HERE."

Ed's voice was barely more than a whisper. He was seated on a bench in front of his locker, bending over to tie a shoe.

Hal was standing next to him, buttoning his uniform shirt.

The locker room was full of players changing into their uniforms for the bus ride to Franklinville. After the game, they would ride back in their uniforms, then shower and change in their own locker room.

Hal looked around. No, he didn't see Warner. "Maybe he didn't know we were excused from the last class so we'd have enough time for the trip to Franklinville."

Ed shook his head. "Blaine and Freddie are here. If they knew, Warner knew. You can bet on it."

"Yeah." Hal knew Ed was right.

Hal glanced at Blaine and Freddie. They were somberly

pulling on their uniforms, Blaine buttoning his shirt, Freddie buckling his belt.

"Did you see him today?" Hal asked. "Maybe he's sick."

"He was here this morning. I saw him in the hall."

Coach Mavis entered and walked through the locker room, saying, "Hustle it up. Let's go. We've got to hit the road."

Did he know that Warner was missing? Maybe so, maybe not. Either way, he said nothing and showed nothing as he made his circle of the locker room and walked out the door.

The players began to close their lockers and drift toward the door.

When Blaine and Freddie walked past, Hal wanted to ask them about Warner, but he said nothing. Warner was no friend of his, and neither were Blaine and Freddie.

But Ed spoke up. "Where's Warner?"

Blaine said only, "He's not coming," and he and Freddie kept walking.

Hal and Ed followed them out of the school to the bus waiting for them in the parking lot.

Coach Mavis was standing at the bus door with a clipboard, checking off the players as they boarded.

Freddie climbed aboard, but when Blaine started to step up the coach tapped his arm and said, "Wait here a minute." Blaine stepped aside while Hal, Ed, and others behind them boarded the bus.

"Something's up," Ed said.

"Uh-huh."

They walked past Freddie and found a pair of empty seats near the rear.

Hal and everyone else watched Coach Mavis talking to Blaine outside the bus. Then Blaine got on the bus and Freddie moved over into the window seat to make room for him. Blaine said something to Freddie, and Freddie nodded in return. Coach Mavis stepped onto the bus, stood for a moment looking at the players, then said something to the driver and sat down.

The bus pulled out of the parking lot.

Hal settled into his seat, chin on his fist, staring out the window as the bus moved through Cannon City and then onto the highway toward Franklinville. His mind kept replaying Warner's remark: "Well, that explains everything, doesn't it?"

For the first few minutes, Ed poured out a stream of chatter about Warner: "You don't suppose—" "Would he really—" "Even Warner isn't dumb enough—" "This is a fine time to—" "Doesn't he care—"

Ed was assuming that Warner was not ill or confused about the hour of departure; he had simply decided not to play.

Hal agreed with Ed's conclusion but let all of Ed's

speculation go unanswered. When Hal failed to respond, Ed eventually settled into silence.

With only the occasional bounce of the bus to interrupt, Hal let his thoughts wander back to the morning. He had arrived at Cannon City High wondering if his world had changed because his father had showed up at practice, and now the secret was out.

Were some of the players suddenly going to act like good friends, or gawk in awe like the players at Blodgett High? Were some going to think that Hal Stevens, the little guy playing second base, considered himself pretty big stuff? Or were they going to think that Hal was getting special treatment because the coach was a friend of his father's?

Through the morning Hal had seen Ed, Rich, and Jason, as well as Harry Small and a couple of other players, but nobody had mentioned his father.

Through lunch period and the afternoon classes, there had been no sign of a problem, either. By the time Hal left his last class and headed for the locker room, he was breathing more easily.

He met Coach Mavis in the hall outside the locker room. "It was good seeing your father," the coach said. "And it was good that he was able to see you play, even if it was just in practice."

Hal had given a little nod and smiled. "He said he'd try

to make it back for a game, especially if we get into the state tournament."

"I hope so."

Coach Mavis had spoken easily, as if everyone had always known that Hal's father was Ralph Stevens, and Hal walked into the locker room feeling like smiling or maybe even whistling: All was right with the world, plus he had a baseball game against the Franklinville Falcons coming up.

But then the world went wrong! The team's heaviest hitter had failed to show up, and the obvious reason was that he was angry and frustrated over the newcomer named Hal Stevens playing second base in his place, and doing it—in Warner's eyes—because of a famous father.

Hal stared at the trees and fence posts flashing past the window of the bus.

When the Gunners' bus pulled into the lot alongside the diamond at Franklinville High, the Falcons were on the field. The infielders were scooping up grounders and firing the ball around the infield. The outfielders were gathering in high flies. Two pitchers were throwing just beyond the first-base line. A smattering of fans were seated in the wooden bleachers.

Coach Mavis stepped off the bus and stood by the door as the players disembarked.

Even though all the players on the bus must have

known by then that Warner Dawson was missing, nobody said anything. But Hal saw plenty of questioning glances—among the players themselves and at Coach Mavis—as they filed off the bus. The coach said nothing and showed nothing.

The players walked from the bus to the bench behind the third-base line, and the Falcons began jogging off the field to make way for the Gunners' pregame warm-up.

When the last of the players had left the bus, Coach Mavis walked across the diamond and greeted the Franklinville coach. Then he cut back across the infield to the third-base side, where his players were doing their stretching exercises.

They seemed to be waiting for him to say something. For most of them, Warner's absence was a mystery. Although Blaine and Freddie surely knew what had happened, they said nothing and nobody asked.

But all Coach Mavis said was, "Let's go. The field is ours."

Hal wondered briefly if Warner might be on his way, but then he remembered Blaine's words to Ed in the locker room: "He's not coming."

It wasn't until after the pregame warm-up, just before the start of the game, that Coach Mavis called the players around him at the bench. "Warner's not here," he said simply. He paused, but instead of elaborating, he nodded to Bud Delaney, a sophomore outfielder who had seen only pinch-hit duty a couple of times, and said, "Bud, you'll start in right field." Then he glanced around at the other players and added, "This will change our batting order, so pay attention."

Chapter 14

IT TOOK NO MORE than the first inning to illustrate the importance of Warner Dawson's big bat to the offense of the Cannon City Gunners.

Hal, leading off, worked the pitcher for a walk. Then Jason rapped the first pitch to left field for a long single, advancing Hal to second.

Blaine stepped to the plate, batting third in place of Ed, who was hitting cleanup in place of Warner.

Hal danced a couple of steps off second base. Jason was edging out from first.

The Franklinville pitcher, so suddenly in deep trouble with two on base and no outs, whirled and threw to first base. Jason leaped back safely. Hal held his ground. The throw to first may have been less an attempt to pick off Jason than an effort to tempt Hal into breaking for third base.

Blaine stepped out of the box, then back in, and the

pitcher went to work, trying to settle down after giving up a walk and a single.

With both the pitcher and Blaine in his line of vision, Hal wished that it was Ed at the plate with Warner on deck, rather than Blaine hitting with Ed on deck. Blaine was not the hitter Ed was, and Ed wasn't the hitter that Warner was. The Gunners' one-two power punch at the plate was lowered not one notch but two with the absence of Warner Dawson. Warner's slot in the batting order had not even come up yet, and already his big bat was being missed.

Blaine fouled off a pitch. He was clearly swinging late, on purpose. A right-handed batter, he was trying to aim his shot to right field to improve Hal's chances of making it safely to third base. Ed, with more power, would have been swinging from the heels in this situation. And, being a left-handed batter with a strong tendency to pull the ball, he probably would have sent it to right field without having to swing late.

Blaine watched a pitch for a called second strike, and then let an outside pitch go by for ball one.

The next pitch came in low, just below his waist, over the outside edge of the plate, and Blaine swung. Again, he was pointing toward right field.

He got his bat on only part of the ball and sent a bouncer toward the second baseman.

108

Hal broke into a sprint for third the instant he saw that the ball was on the ground. Head down as he ran, he glanced up and saw the third baseman, his foot on the bag, glove up, waiting. Hal had no way of knowing what was happening behind him. Surely the second baseman had fielded the ball without trouble: The bouncer didn't have much power behind it. Now he was throwing it to somebody.

Hal leaped into a headfirst slide for third base. If the second baseman had flipped the ball to the shortstop at second base to put out Jason, Hal was no longer in force-out danger. The third baseman would have to tag him to put him out.

But the ball never came to third base.

Hal, with his hand on the bag, looked around to see the first baseman take in the throw from the shortstop seconds before Blaine's foot hit the bag—a double play.

The Falcons had chosen a sure two outs and a runner on third rather than risk leaving themselves with only one out and runners on first and second with Ed coming to bat. Hal thought that if he had been the Falcons' second baseman he probably would have gone for the runner heading for third. But maybe the Falcons' second baseman was right.

Hal got to his feet and dusted himself off as Ed stepped into the batter's box.

The pitcher looked at Hal at third and took a deep breath. He wasn't out of danger yet, but he was two outs closer to safety.

Hal looked back at Ed, who was glaring at the pitcher with his bat cocked. If Ed had been the third batter, as he should have been, he surely would have gotten the ball out of the infield. It might have been an out, but not a double play. And a long fly to right field, even if it had been caught, might have advanced Hal to third base with only one out.

Ed swung and missed, then poled the next pitch high into right field.

The Franklinville outfielder backed up and caught it.

Without Warner Dawson, the Gunners ended the inning with one hit, one base on balls, one left on base—and no runs.

Thanks to Freddie Harrison's spectacular diving catch of a line drive with two on and two out, the Gunners survived the top of the Falcon's batting order in the first inning without giving up a run.

But Hal saw enough slugging power in the first five batters to understand how the Franklinville team had averaged nine runs a game in their first four games. Fly balls went deep, deep into the outfield. Line drives, like the one Freddie speared, seemed to whistle. Even the grounder that Hal fielded for the side's second out thumped into his glove with more punch than he could remember from any other ground ball.

When Freddie rolled over from his diving catch and held his left hand in the air—the ball in the glove—Hal ran over to him, shouting "Great! Great!" as he ran.

Freddie, back on his feet, was grinning. This had been one of those catches that either happened or didn't. There was no time to think, to weigh choices, to make a decision. Suddenly the rocketing ball was there, and the fielder either got his glove on it, or he didn't. Freddie's instinct had sent him into a dive, gloved hand extended.

Freddie slapped hands with Hal and they started toward the bench.

Larry Milford, coming off the mound, heaved a sigh of relief. As he walked, he looked back at Freddie and nodded. He didn't grin or shout or even speak. The nod said it all. Freddie had saved the left-hander from giving up one, maybe two runs on the hit.

As they approached the bench, Coach Mavis said something to Larry and then walked across and gave Freddie a pat on the back.

Hal sat on the bench next to Ed and watched three Gunners go down in order—a pop fly to the second baseman, a grounder to the third baseman, and a strikeout.

* * *

In the bottom of the third inning the Franklinville pitcher was the leadoff hitter, and behind him loomed the top of the Franklinville lineup—the menacing parade of five sluggers.

Larry, who relied more on control than on speed, seldom struck anyone out. But he could put the ball where he wanted it to go, and he rarely walked a batter. He kept the ball low, trying to force the weak-hitting pitcher to hit on the ground. Better that than a lucky poke over an infielder's head for a single.

Hal moved forward a few steps. He figured that the pitcher, a right-handed batter, might hit the ball in his direction, but not with much authority.

With the count two balls and two strikes, the pitcher swung awkwardly and sent the ball bouncing to Hal's right.

Hal moved over, caught the ball at the top of a bounce, and threw him out.

On the mound, Larry removed his cap and wiped perspiration from his forehead. One down. But the heavy hitters were coming up.

"Mow 'em down!" Hal shouted.

Ed and Blaine both advanced halfway to the mound and called out encouragement.

The first batter in the Falcons' hitting order looked strong, carried a big bat, and handled it easily. Last time at bat, he had backed up Jason in deep center field.

Coach Mavis was on his feet at the bench. He made a little waving motion, signaling the infielders to back off from the forward positions they had taken for the weak-hitting pitcher. But Ed, Hal, Freddie, and Blaine were already taking a couple of steps backward.

Larry fed the hitter two pitches low and on the outside, one for a ball, one a called strike. Then he sent a fastball in, chest high, and the batter swung and missed.

On the next pitch, waist high on the outside edge of the plate, the batter swung and smashed the ball on a line to deep left center field. By the time Jason chased down the ball and threw it to Hal, the batter was on second base with a stand-up double.

The next batter sent a hard grounder to Blaine at third base. Blaine got his glove on it, brought the ball up, hesitated a moment to hold the runner at second, and threw out the batter at first.

"Way to go!" Hal called out.

Two down, and Larry had his cap off again, wiping his forehead. The Falcons were hitting him, and hitting him hard, but so far they weren't getting any runs for their work.

Then the next batter rapped a long single down the line in right field, scoring the runner from second; and the cleanup hitter promptly poled the first pitch over the fence in left field for a home run.

Coach Mavis walked to the mound and spoke with

Larry, then returned to the bench, leaving him in.

The next batter popped up to Freddie, and the Falcons finished the inning with a 3–0 lead.

The Gunners narrowed the edge to 3–2 in the top of the fifth when Ed homered with Blaine on base, and the Falcons promptly answered by piling on two more runs in their half of the inning.

Larry left the mound after giving up consecutive doubles in the Falcons' rally, and Rich came on and cut them down with his blistering fastball.

In the top of the ninth, with the Gunners still trailing by 5–2, Hal was the leadoff hitter.

Hal took one pitch outside for a ball, and Coach Mavis signaled for a bunt. Hal nodded his understanding. It made sense. The Franklinville pitcher, who had gone the distance, was showing signs of weariness. He was going to leap less quickly at a slow roller. The catcher, too, had had a long afternoon. The third baseman was playing back in his normal position, obviously not expecting a bunt.

Hal waggled his bat like a power hitter when the next pitch came in, right down the middle and just below the shoulders for a called strike.

The third pitch was perfect for Hal, waist high and a bit soft. He turned his body to face the pitcher, slid his right hand down the bat, and gave the ball a slight poke. The ball dropped to the ground and rolled.

Hal dropped the bat and raced for first base, and the Falcons' startled third baseman lunged forward.

Hal crossed first base and then heard the ball thump into the first baseman's mitt. Safe.

But there he stayed as first Jason fouled out, and then Blaine lined out to the shortstop.

Ed strode to the plate—the Gunners' last hope.

He watched an outside pitch for a ball, then took a called strike. He swung on the next pitch and sent a scorching grounder to the right of the first baseman.

Hal broke into a sprint for second base on the slim chance the Falcons' first baseman would let Ed's hard-hit grounder get past him.

But the first baseman reached across, caught the ball, and stepped over and touched the base with his foot, ending the game.

Hal crossed second base, then turned and jogged across the infield toward the bench. The players were gathering there, picking up their gloves and jackets. Hal saw Coach Mavis make his way toward home plate to shake hands with the Franklinville coach. He was stopped several times by Franklinville players wanting to shake the hand of the former All-Star shortstop.

Hal and Ed came together in front of the bench.

"We should've beaten those guys," Ed said angrily.

Hal nodded, knowing that Ed meant the Gunners owed their first defeat of the season to the absence of Warner Dawson's bat.

Chapter 15

THE ANGRY WORDS THAT erupted on the bus taking the team back to Cannon City High began with Ed grumbling to Hal.

Coach Mavis had just completed a tour down the aisle, leaning in toward the seated players with a compliment here, a word of consolation there, an occasional pat on the shoulder.

To Hal, he said, "You played well. That bunt in the ninth was a beauty."

And to Ed, "Good game. You came through with a big hit when we needed it."

"Not in the ninth," Ed said.

Coach Mavis gave him a grin and said, "Nobody homers every time, Ed."

Watching the coach walk back up the aisle to his seat at the front of the bus, Hal marveled that the former major-league shortstop considered the high school game important. Don Mavis had played in World Series and All-

Star games. He had batted and fielded line drives, flies, and grounders in the fever of a National League pennant race. How could he consider the Cannon City High Gunners' loss to the Franklinville Falcons important? But he did.

As the coach sat down behind the driver, Hal's thoughts were interrupted by Ed. "Warner really let us down, and all because of his ego—nothing else," he said.

"Yeah, I guess."

"There's more to it than just this one game," Ed added. "Everybody loses once in a while. But we started the season with a chance to go a long way—maybe all the way—in the state tournament. And Warner has junked it all. His hitting is—was—an important part of our strength. We saw that today. But he's junked it."

"Uh-huh," Hal said. "Well, maybe he'll change his mind and come back." Hal did not think the odds of Warner's returning were very good. Coming back and admitting that he had made a mistake probably would be harder to swallow than staying on the team in the first place.

Ed seemed to pick up on the lack of conviction in Hal's voice. He looked at him and said only, "Nah!"

Hal turned and stared out the window at the deepening darkness. He didn't want Ed to pursue his point. He didn't want to think that the Gunners had lost their heaviest hitter because he had happened to show up, and the coach wanted him—Ralph Stevens's son, the "coach's pet"—to replace Warner at second base.

But Ed continued. "In the first inning, my fly to deep right would have advanced you to third with one out and Warner coming up—if Blaine hadn't already hit into a double play."

Hal couldn't argue with Ed's reasoning. He'd had the same thoughts himself at the time. But he turned to Ed and said, "Yes—*if.* But how do you know you wouldn't have hit the same pitch Blaine hit, and bounced into a double play, if you'd been batting third in place of Blaine?" Hal did not believe it, but he hoped the question would quiet Ed.

Others were glancing around—Blaine and Freddie in seats one row forward and across the aisle, Harry Small directly across the aisle, Larry Milford in front of them. Ed wasn't speaking loudly, but he wasn't making any effort to keep his voice down either.

Hal hoped nobody else joined in.

Then Ed abruptly leaned into the aisle and said to Blaine, "Your buddy let us all down, you know. We needed him."

Freddie said sharply, "Lay off."

Blaine glared at Ed and said, "You're the one who made the last out of the game."

Ed snapped, "I didn't hit into any double plays."

Others were turning to see what was happening.

Larry rose from his seat, turned, and said, "Cut it out. Forget it."

Ed shrugged at Larry. "It's just that their big-shot buddy let us down because he got his feelings hurt."

Blaine said softly, "Warner can take care of his own business."

Hal looked at Blaine, surprised that he neither took another verbal swing at Ed nor rose to loud defense of Warner. Blaine looked back at Hal, his face showing nothing.

By this time Coach Mavis was making his way down the aisle. "What's the problem?" he asked of no one in particular.

There was a long moment of silence. Then Ed said, "Nothing."

The others seemed willing to let that stand for their answer.

Coach Mavis looked around and then returned to his seat.

Hal glanced at Ed. He was slumped back, staring straight ahead. Larry had dropped back into his seat in front of them, and across the aisle Blaine and Freddie were sitting rigidly, eyes to the front. Hal shifted in his seat, almost turning his back to Ed, and resumed staring out the window. He wished the bus would speed up. Maybe those lights in the distance were Cannon City.

In the locker room, neither Ed nor any of the other players mentioned Warner, or the flare-up. Everyone seemed strangely subdued.

Ed was far from his usual cheerful self. He should have been putting the loss behind him with a laugh, promising to wipe out the Falcons next time. But he seemed genuinely angry, and determined to stay that way. Blaine and Freddie—and, of course, Warner—had always maintained an air of self-importance. After all, they were starters for the third year. But now Blaine and Freddie looked like anything but rulers of the roost. And Warner—what was he acting like at this moment?

Coach Mavis made a quick tour of the locker room, nodding and speaking to the players getting into their street clothes in front of their lockers. Maybe, Hal thought, the coach was making sure that any hint of trouble had been left behind on the bus.

Hal, now dressed, pulled on his jacket, scooped his books out of the bottom of the locker, and closed the door, spinning the combination lock. He turned to Ed. "Catching the bus?"

Ed, still dressing, said, "Sure, give me a minute."

Hal sat down on a bench while Ed stuffed his shirttail into his jeans and buckled his belt. He watched Blaine and Freddie leave the dressing room together, then others.

The dressing room was almost empty when Ed closed

his locker and said, "Ready." They walked out together.

Outside, on the two-block walk through the darkness to Ridgeway Avenue, Hal said, "I never saw you pop off like that."

Ed took a couple of steps before he answered. "Those three guys have always acted like such big shots. Last year, when I was riding the bench, they barely spoke to me." He turned to Hal. "You saw the same thing yourself this year when you showed up."

"Uh-huh."

"So then you beat out Warner for second base and—just like that!—he decides to quit. It's like, you know, if he can't be king, he won't play. I just think it's pretty low. And I figured that Blaine and Freddie—they're just as bad as Warner, you know—might as well know what I think."

Hal walked along without speaking.

Then Ed said, "You know that Warner was calling you 'coach's pet,' don't you?"

"Yeah, I heard him."

"Well, you're a better second baseman than he ever dreamed of being."

"But he's a better hitter."

Hal could almost hear Ed's grin. "Yeah," Ed said, "he is."

The bus ride home in the early evening was a quick one. The rush hour was long since past. There were only a half-dozen other passengers, and the driver zipped past most stops without even a pause. Automobile traffic was also light, because this was the dinner hour in most of the homes of Cannon City.

Hal was glad that this was Friday and that the weekend stretched ahead—and that Monday, with its return to Cannon City High, was two days away. Two days of reprieve, Hal figured.

On Monday, Warner Dawson—and probably Blaine Wilkins and Freddie Harrison, too—would be explaining why Warner had quit the team. Everyone would be wondering, so Warner was going to be ready to tell them. And "coach's pet" were the first words Hal expected Warner to say.

He expected him to say other things, too. Such as: "Turns out, you know, that he's Ralph Stevens's son, and his father is an old buddy of Coach Mavis's." And: "He couldn't play third base—didn't have the arm for it—so his father's old friend found another position for him." Warner was bound to wind up with something like: "Well, that's the way things work, you know, when you've got a famous father who's a friend of the coach. Only thing is, I don't have to put up with it, and so I'm not."

Hal knew that Ed, and maybe Rich and Jason, too, might be there for the defense. But the veteran starters—Blaine and Freddie—were going to be difficult to shut up.

Monday, Hal figured, might be tense.

The bus was approaching Hal's stop. He pulled the cord above his head, got up, and walked to the front door. The driver swerved the bus to the curb and slowed to a halt. The door opened and Hal stepped out.

As he walked the block to the apartment house, Hal managed to put the imagined voice of Warner Dawson out of his mind.

"I'm home," he called as he stepped through the front doorway into the living room. He dropped his books on a chair and began taking off his jacket.

"Who won?" his mother asked from around the corner in the kitchen.

Hal dropped his jacket on top of the books and walked through the living room and into the kitchen. The table was set, and dinner seemed to be awaiting his arrival. That was fine with him. It had been a long time since lunch. "We lost," Hal said.

"Too bad. How'd it go with you?"

"Okay. I did okay."

Ellen Stevens opened the refrigerator and got a carton of milk. "Freddie Harrison wants you to call him," she said as she began pouring a glass for Hal.

Chapter 16

HAL STOOD IN THE darkness in front of the apartment house, not knowing what to expect. When he had returned Freddie's call after dinner, the conversation had been weird.

"Freddie, this is Hal," he had begun.

"Oh?" Freddie said. That was all. Nothing else.

Hal felt his face flush. Freddie sounded surprised, even indifferent. Had his mother made a mistake in taking the message? Or was somebody playing a joke on him?

"My mother said you called."

"Oh, yeah. That was an hour ago."

Hal pursed his lips. Get real, he said to himself. Am I supposed to drop everything and rush to the phone the instant I'm told I have a message to call Freddie Harrison? But aloud Hal said, "Yeah, I ate my dinner first."

"Okay, it was nothing urgent."

"What's up?"

"We need to talk to you—about Warner quitting the team."

"We?" Hal asked. What was Freddie Harrison, who barely acknowledged Hal's existence, getting at?

"Yeah. Blaine and me."

A question raced through Hal's mind. Were Warner's friends going to ask, or maybe even demand, that Hal step aside or even quit the team to clear the way for Warner to return to second base for his senior season?

"What have you got on your mind?"

"It isn't something we can discuss on the phone. Can you meet us tonight?"

"Tonight?"

"It's important."

First Freddie says the call wasn't urgent. Now it's important. Well, okay. Maybe this is Freddie's way of trying to manipulate things. Hal tried to sort out his thoughts quickly. He didn't want to meet with Freddie and Blaine, especially when he had no idea what they were trying to pull off. And he wondered, too, if Warner would be there. Finally, he shrugged. He knew that he would have to listen to them sometime—tonight, tomorrow, Sunday, or, worst of all, on Monday at school.

"Blaine has his car. We'll pick you up in about fifteen minutes. Okay?"

Hal had the uncomfortable feeling that he was being pulled into something not of his own making by two team-

126

mates—three, if Warner showed up—who were not his friends. Nevertheless, he said, "Okay."

After giving Freddie his address and hanging up, he turned to see his mother coming into the living room.

"I couldn't help hearing," she said. "What was that all about?"

"A problem with someone on the team. Doesn't really involve me, but a couple of the guys want to talk about it."

"Don't be late, okay?"

"Okay."

Hal went to his room to get his jacket. He thought of calling Ed. He might have some idea of what was up, and how to handle it. But, no, Hal decided. Ed didn't like Warner and his crowd, so he might try to argue that Hal should not listen to them. Or, worse yet, he might insist on joining in the meeting.

Hal pulled on his jacket and left.

Hal recognized the car turning the corner under the streetlight as Blaine's, and he stepped to the curb and waved.

When the car slowed to a halt at the curb, Freddie hopped out of the passenger side and got into the back-seat, leaving the front door open for Hal. Hal slid in beside Blaine and closed the door, and Blaine pulled back into the street.

"Bruno's okay?" Blaine asked.

The pizza place outside town on the highway to Peoria wasn't a student hangout, as far as Hal knew, but maybe Freddie and Blaine didn't want to risk running into other teammates.

"Sure, fine," Hal said.

"We've never had much of a chance to talk," Blaine said. "How do you like Cannon City?"

No, not much of a chance to talk, Hal thought, because you and your buddies have always looked straight through me.

"It's fine," Hal said, staring straight ahead. "Cannon City seems okay."

They rode in silence for a couple of blocks.

"That was a real surprise—Ralph Stevens being your father," Blaine said.

Hal didn't answer for a moment. Then he said, "Well, he doesn't live here, you know. He and my mother are divorced. He lives in New York."

"But nobody knew he was your father."

Hal decided to take advantage of the opening. "No, that's not true. Some people knew, but it was no big deal." Let them wonder who knew what they hadn't, he thought. Then he added, "Even Coach Mavis knew it—but I didn't know he knew it. He found out from my student file in the office, but he never said anything to me about it. And I never had a reason to say anything to him about it."

So much for Ralph Stevens's son figuring he was due

special treatment as the coach's pet, Hal thought.

"No kidding," said Blaine.

Hal thought he sounded surprised, maybe even disbelieving. From the backseat, Freddie said nothing, and Blaine drove on without speaking further.

They turned into the parking lot at Bruno's and came to a halt near the front door. Inside, they settled into a booth, Hal on one side of the table, Blaine and Freddie on the other, facing him. At this hour, the dinner crowd had left and the late-night crowd had not yet arrived, so the place was almost empty.

"Want to order a pizza?" Blaine asked.

"Not for me," Hal said. "I just had dinner."

"I'll split a small one with you," Freddie said. It was the first time he had spoken since Hal got into the car.

After the waitress took their order, Blaine immediately turned to Hal. "First of all, there's one thing that needs to be said, just so everybody knows where everybody stands."

Hal kept his eyes on Blaine and waited.

"You're the best second baseman we've got—a really good one, as a matter of fact—and you're exactly where you ought to be, our starting second baseman."

Hal frowned slightly. What's going on here? He looked from Blaine to Freddie. Freddie, wearing a serious expression, nodded his agreement.

"Okay?" Blaine said.

"Okay," Hal said faintly.

Blaine smiled at Hal's confusion and said, "Second, you're the one who can get Warner to come back."

Hal blinked at Blaine. Then he looked at Freddie. Freddie was watching him closely. Hal looked back to Blaine.

His immediate thought was that the idea was crazy. But he was too surprised to speak. Earlier, while he was waiting for them in front of his apartment house, he had tried to imagine what he was walking into. He would never—not in a million years—have come up with this.

Before Hal could respond, Blaine was speaking again.

"We need Warner—his hitting. You saw that today. With his bat in the lineup, we're a really strong team, and we've got a good chance of going a long way in the state tournament. Without him, we're just another team, maybe above average but nothing more. Agreed?"

"Sure, but—" Hal stopped and looked from Blaine to Freddie, and then back to Blaine. Nobody could say that the Gunners didn't need Warner's strong hitting. But why were Warner's friends asking *him* to talk to Warner?

"But what?" Blaine asked.

"Don't you think that it's you guys, not me, who need to talk to Warner?" He looked from one to the other and, not getting an answer, added, "Or Coach Mavis. In fact, maybe Coach Mavis has already talked to him."

Blaine shook his head. "The coach said he would be calling Warner, but that's all. He's not going to pressure him to come back. Freddie and I talked to him in the coaches' office after the game. Coach Mavis thinks it's better that Warner decide to come back, or not, on his own. But he's wrong. The longer Warner stays out, the tougher it will be for him to return."

"Uh-huh, maybe," Hal said.

Blaine and Freddie exchanged glances. Then Blaine said to Freddie, "Go on."

Freddie gave a little nod and, with his arms on the table, leaned in toward Hal. "Blaine and I have tried to talk to Warner all day today, between classes and at lunch—after he told us this morning that he was quitting."

"And he wouldn't change his mind," Hal said.

"Right."

Hal shook his head. "If he wouldn't listen to you, what makes you think he'll listen to me? He and I aren't exactly best friends, you know."

Freddie took a breath and said, "Well, right now I don't think he'll talk to us at all."

"Oh?"

"Blaine and I got fed up with his grumbling. We told him that he ought to face up to the fact that you're better than he is at second, and that he belonged in right field and at the plate."

Hal looked at the two across the table from him. The arrival of the waitress placing a pizza in the center of the table and soda in front of each of them saved him from having to respond immediately. He didn't know what to say. Both Blaine and Freddie thought he deserved the second-base position. Great. Then why had they continued to act as if a great wrong had been done to Warner?

When the waitress left, Blaine picked up the story. "He walked away from us during the lunch period and hasn't spoken to us since. When Freddie called him this evening after the game he refused to come to the phone."

Before Hal could speak, Freddie spoke again. "We know Warner. He flies off the handle, plus he's stubborn. But I'd bet that by now he wants to come back, if he can find the right way to do it."

"And you think I'm the right way?" Hal asked, sounding—and feeling—less than convinced.

Freddie reached for a slice of pizza. "Yes, you," he said.

Hal waited without speaking.

Blaine leaned forward. "Warner knows as well as everyone else that you're better at second than he is. But nobody knew that when Coach Mavis made the change—not Warner, not Freddie, not me—and Warner got mad and said a lot of things that I think he regretted. Freddie and I were telling him to lay off and accept the change as good for the team when—*boom!*—your father shows up and Warner now claims that he was right all along."

Freddie interjected, "Warner feels better telling himself that he lost out at second base because the coach was playing favorites, not because the other second baseman was better."

"But you can bet," Blaine said, "that Warner knows you're better at second than he is."

"And you're the one who can tell him that," Freddie said, "and tell him that we need his hitting in the lineup."

Hal rolled his eyes.

"Think about it," Freddie said. "Okay?"

"Think about it," Freddie had said. And Hal had.

He'd thought about it Friday night after Blaine and Freddie dropped him off in front of the apartment house. He'd thought about it as he and his mother watched television that evening. And he'd thought about it that night in the darkness of his room as he lay motionless on his bed, wide-awake.

The game against the Franklinville Falcons now seemed a year ago. Ed's tirade on the bus seemed only a distant echo. And how long ago was it that Ed had noticed Warner missing from the locker room? Hal could hardly remember.

What made Blaine and Freddie so sure that Hal could talk Warner into coming back? If his two best friends couldn't do it, how could the newcomer who had beaten him out of the second-base position manage it?

During the meeting with Blaine and Freddie at Bruno's, Hal had simply listened, first in astonishment, then with growing uncertainty. He had not made any promises to Blaine and Freddie, and they had not tried to extract any. They seemed to agree that Hal needed—as Freddie put it—to "think about it."

The more Hal thought, the more certain he became that he had to give it a try. There was, of course, the team's obvious need of Warner's hitting. If Hal could do anything to restore that to the Gunners' lineup, he was ready to make the effort. But beyond that, Hal could not escape the fact that he was, at least indirectly, responsible for Warner's quitting. He owed it to the team, and possibly even to Warner, to try and bring him back.

Still, the prospect scared him. Would Warner even agree to talk to him? And if he did, what would Hal say?

This was one of those times—there seemed to be a lot of them—when Hal wished his father was around. They might take a walk, and talk. His father was a man, and also a baseball player, and might know what Hal should do.

Hal briefly weighed the possibility of discussing the matter with Ed. But Ed didn't like Warner and his friends, and surely he would only try to talk Hal out of making any move at all. No, there was nothing to be gained by asking Ed for advice.

Just before he dropped off to sleep, Hal decided to telephone the man he felt he'd only begun to get to know over dinner at the Leland House restaurant.

Chapter 17

ED CALLED JUST AS Hal and his mother were finishing breakfast. He, Jason, Rich, and a couple of others were going to Peoria for an electronics show. Did Hal want to go?

Hal hesitated. He didn't know when he might be able to reach his father. If Ralph Stevens was out of town, or even just out on a golf course, Hal would have to leave a message and wait, or place the call again later. Also, he wanted to get the visit with Warner behind him today, if possible. "I'd better not," Hal said. "I've got some things I have to do."

As he hung up and returned to the dining table, Ellen was watching him. "It sounds like you've got a busy day," she said.

Hal drank the rest of the milk in his glass and then said, "It's a problem with one of the players—the same one I met with Freddie Harrison and Blaine Wilkins about last night." He added, "Ed and the others aren't involved."

"Oh."

Hal took a deep breath and said, "I need to call Dad. Will it be all right?" He knew his mother would say yes, and he hoped she wouldn't ask about the problem that required a telephone conversation with his father.

But Ellen said only, "Of course." She got up and began carrying dishes into the kitchen. Hal picked up his plate and glass and followed her. "I've got some shopping to do," she said. "Why don't you call while I'm gone."

Hal smiled at her. "Thanks."

Gloria answered the phone.

"This is Hal. Is Dad there?"

While he responded to Gloria's greeting and then waited for his father to come to the phone, Hal tried to sort out the thoughts racing through his mind. How do you tell your father that the fact he is your father is a problem? Hal knew he was going to have to say it and ask advice about how to handle the problem. He kept telling himself that the man he had had dinner with at the Leland House restaurant—a man he now realized he'd never really known before—would understand, and would help.

"Hal?" Ralph Stevens's voice coming out of the receiver registered concern. Hal seldom telephoned his father, and this call, coming so close on the heels of their visit, seemed to have set off alarm bells. "Is anything wrong?"

136

"No." Then Hal added, "Well, yes. I've got a problem I need to talk to you about." He could not have said that to his father a week ago. Even now, it sounded strange to him. He took a breath and said, "Do you have time to—"

"Sure." Ralph sounded concerned, but the hint of alarm was gone.

Hal began immediately. "Our strongest hitter has quit the team because of me."

"You?"

"He played second base the last two years, and Don Mavis shifted him to right field to put me in at second. The guy says the coach is playing favorites"—Hal hesitated—"because I'm your son."

Ralph Stevens said nothing for a moment. Hal wondered if this was the first time it had ever occurred to him that his fame might have an impact on his son. Finally, he said, "I see."

Hal continued, "A couple of his friends think I can talk him into coming back to the team."

"They may be right."

"But I don't know what to say."

Hal waited through a few moments of silence. His father was thinking. Then there would be words of advice.

But instead Ralph Stevens abruptly asked, "Has this sort of thing—being my son—been a problem for you before?"

Hal bit his lip. Then he said, "Sometimes."

Again, silence. Finally, "Is this why you were making the point to me in a big way how really pleased you were to be playing second base instead of third—to get out from under my shadow?"

Hal waited before answering. So his father had seen through his announcement over dinner that he liked playing second base. Well, Hal had wanted truth-telling time with his father, and here it was. "Yes," he said, "it's better being Hal Stevens than Ralph Stevens's son."

In the silence that followed, Hal stared at a small vase on the edge of the desk. What was his father going to say?

"Hal, I never realized that this was a problem for you."

"I can handle it."

"I'm sure you can. I'm sure you've been handling it."

Hal said nothing.

"Now your teammate…"

"Yes?"

"Maybe you should tell him that being Ralph Stevens's son is not an advantage. To the contrary, it's sometimes a disadvantage. Your teammate is the lucky one, not you."

Hal smiled. "No, I'm lucky."

In the early afternoon, Hal steered his mother's car to the curb in front of Warner Dawson's house and came to a stop. He sat there for a moment, looking at the house. Inside, Warner Dawson was waiting. Or, at least, he had said he would be. On the phone Hal had announced simply, "I'm coming over to talk to you." Warner had replied, "About what?"

Hal answered, "You know what. Will you be there?"

Warner said only, "All right."

In the yard across the street a man was cutting the grass. In a driveway on this side of the street, a young man and woman were washing a car.

Hal took a deep breath and got out of the car. He walked up the driveway and the three stone steps to the wide porch, and across the porch to the front door. He pushed the doorbell.

After what seemed like an hour to Hal, the door opened.

Warner looked at Hal in silence.

Hal said, "Hi," and felt like a fool.

Warner nodded slightly. He opened the screen door and stepped out. "My folks are inside," he said. "We can talk out here."

Hal let out a long breath as he stepped back to make way for Warner. Hal had made it to first base—a long way from scoring, but not called out so far.

"It's not easy being Ralph Stevens's son," Hal said.

The two boys were seated side by side on the top step of the stone porch.

Hal, elbows on knees, hands clasped, did not look at Warner. He stared straight ahead as he spoke, out over the lawn toward the house across the street.

"Is that right?" Warner said.

Hal hesitated, trying to measure the degree of sarcasm. He still did not look at Warner, but he could imagine the half-sneer on his face. He took a deep breath and plunged ahead.

"Did you know that Ralph Stevens's son had to play third base, and had to be a heavy hitter? But that Hal Stevens can play second base, and can place his hits and bunt for singles?"

Warner looked at Hal. "What?"

"While you were thinking that Coach Mavis put you in right field to open up second base for the son of an old friend and baseball celebrity, I was thinking that the son of Ralph Stevens had failed. Oh, I knew I wasn't going to beat Blaine at third base long before Coach Mavis moved me to second. And I thought, Well, playing second base is better than not playing at all. But I didn't feel good about it—not at first."

Hal glanced sideways at Warner. He hoped Freddie had been right when he'd said that Warner wanted to come back to the team, and just needed somebody to give him a way to do it. But Warner's profile as he stared straight ahead offered no clues.

"Then, after the first game, I knew that I didn't have to

140

play third base like Ralph Stevens. I'm Hal Stevens, a second baseman. I knew that I didn't have to be a slugger like my famous father. I'm Hal Stevens, with a light bat."

Hal took a deep breath.

"Everyone always compared my play to my father's, and I never measured up—until the day I realized that I was Hal Stevens instead of Ralph Stevens's son."

Hal waited. Not a word or even a slight movement from Warner. Well, Hal told himself, here comes the part that will probably send Warner stomping back into his house.

"But you"—Hal paused and then repeated the word—"you want me to go on being the son of Ralph Stevens instead of being me, just plain Hal Stevens."

Warner swung his head around. Hal couldn't tell whether Warner's eyes were showing anger or puzzlement. Either way, he made no move to get to his feet.

Hal plunged on. "You called me 'coach's pet' without any reason. And then the other day when my father showed up, you thought you had found the reason. And you liked the idea because now you could tell yourself that I beat you out at second base because I'm Ralph Stevens's son. Well, Warner, I beat you out because I'm Hal Stevens. And you might as well face the fact."

No doubt, the look in Warner's eyes was anger, not puzzlement. Still, he did not get up and walk away.

"You're our heaviest hitter. With you in the lineup,

we'll win a lot of games. Without you, we'll lose some that we should've won. The Franklinville game, for one." He paused, then said, "We all want you back. But you're going to have to accept me as Hal Stevens, not as the son of Ralph Stevens. And Hal Stevens is going to keep on playing second base."

Hal stood up and looked down at Warner. He managed a small smile—a smile he didn't really feel—and said, "See, it's not easy being Ralph Stevens's son. I'm always having to explain something to somebody."

He walked toward the car. "See you around," he said without looking back.

Chapter 18

A LIGHT RAIN, BARELY more than a mist, was falling as Hal walked the couple of blocks from the bus stop to the school on Monday morning. Glancing at the clouds, he wondered if the weather might force Coach Mavis to cancel practice. That might give Warner an excuse to delay his decision one more day. By then, the Gunners would be taking the field against the Knightstown High Tigers. Hal turned up the collar of his jacket and jogged the last half-block to the school.

Pulling open the front door and stepping inside, Hal found himself almost face-to-face with Warner.

The lobby and hallway were full of students milling around before the bell.

Hal, wondering if Warner was waiting there for him, stopped and gave him a questioning look. Warner gave Hal a slight nod and walked on without speaking.

Hal, puzzled, nodded back.

Turning and heading toward the hall, Hal saw Freddie,

Blaine, and some other seniors across the lobby. Maybe Warner was still mad at them.

Was that a bad sign? Well, it wasn't good, that's for sure.

Hal walked on toward his locker, thinking how strange it was that for these last few days his life had been dominated by a big-shot senior who never spoke to or even seemed to look at him.

On Saturday afternoon, Hal had barely returned home from Warner's place when Freddie called. "Have you seen him?" Freddie wanted to know.

The timing of the call was such that Hal wondered if Warner had called Freddie. It didn't seem likely, but it was possible. "Yes," Hal said finally. "Did he call you after I left?"

"No, I haven't talked to him." Then, "What did he say?"

Hal found that easy to answer. "Almost nothing," he said.

"But he listened to you?"

Although Hal would not have phrased it that way, he said, "I guess so. At least he sat there while I talked."

"Oh."

"Yeah. Well, anyway, I tried. Now it's up to him."

"What did you say to him?"

"It's hard to repeat. Let's just wait and see what Warner does."

Not fifteen minutes later, Blaine called. "Freddie says you saw Warner."

"Uh-huh," Hal said, and then repeated what he had told Freddie.

When he hung up, he dialed Ed's house and left a message for Ed to call when he returned from Peoria. Maybe Ed and some of the guys would like to go to a movie tonight. But Hal resolved not to mention his talk with Warner.

Hal didn't bump into Warner, Blaine, or Freddie all morning. This was not unusual, but, still, he was glad none of them popped up in front of him in the halls.

By noon the misty rain had blown away, to be replaced by a blue, cloudless sky.

At lunch, Hal ate with Ed, Rich, and Larry. He spotted Blaine, Freddie, and a couple of their friends at a table at the other end of the cafeteria. To his surprise, he saw Warner carry his tray from the food counter over to them. Then Warner said something, Freddie answered, and Warner put his tray on the table and sat down.

Was that a good sign? Well, it couldn't be a bad sign.

Only a few days ago, the picture of the three seniors together at a cafeteria table had served only to remind Hal that he was a newcomer, excluded and ignored. But now two of those seniors—Blaine and Freddie—had tried to be friendly. Maybe that was only because they felt they needed him. But, still, they were friendly, and they had admitted that Hal deserved the second-base position. And Warner? Well, he had at least listened to Hal. Maybe.

When Hal and his friends had finished eating and had gotten up to return their trays to the rack, he watched Blaine and Freddie, hoping for some indication that Warner had told them he had decided to return to the team. But he couldn't catch either boy's eye. All he saw was the back of Warner's head, Freddie talking, and Blaine watching both of them.

Hal piled his tray on top of the others on the rack and walked out of the cafeteria with his friends.

Hal and Jason came out of the last class of the day and met Ed in the hall, and the three of them headed toward the stairs leading to the locker room.

"Has anyone heard anything about Warner?" Ed asked.

Hal looked at Ed. Had he heard about Hal's visit to Warner's house? No, probably not.

Jason said, "Not me."

"I haven't either," Hal said.

"He's a jerk," Ed said.

At the bottom of the stairs they turned and walked toward the locker-room door. Ahead of them, Lew Webster, the left fielder, waved as he went through the doorway.

Hal felt a sudden twinge of anxiety. What if he walked

into the locker room and Warner was there, changing into his uniform as if nothing had happened? What if Blaine and Freddie were there with him, all three of them joking and laughing, as if the last three days had not happened? What was Hal supposed to do—shake Warner's hand and welcome him back? And what if Warner looked right through or past him? Hal took a breath.

The first person Hal saw when he walked in the room was Coach Mavis. The coach smiled. "Good afternoon," he said.

Ed said, "Hi, coach," and Hal nodded, and then they walked over to their lockers.

Across the room, Blaine and Freddie were peeling off their shirts. Warner was nowhere in sight.

Hal opened his locker and got out his uniform, but he was looking at Blaine and Freddie as he changed. They owed him some word on what had transpired in the cafeteria. For a moment he considered walking across and asking.

Then Blaine looked at him—a blank, expressionless look—and shook his head slowly. Freddie turned, looked at Hal, and shrugged.

Did that mean that Warner was not coming back? Or that they just didn't know? Either way, it was obvious the two weren't expecting their friend to walk through the door at any minute. Warner clearly had not bent under whatever urgings had taken place at the lunch table.

Hal pulled off his shirt and hung it in the locker, then put on a sweatshirt and his uniform shirt. He stepped out of his jeans and into uniform pants.

Why had Warner bothered to listen to him? Why would Warner shun Blaine and Freddie, and then have lunch with them? Nothing made sense.

Hal was bending over, tying a shoe, when Ed said, "Hey!"

Hal looked up and saw Warner crossing the locker room to Coach Mavis. Hal straightened and watched. Then he looked around the room. By now, everyone was watching.

Coach Mavis was greeting Warner the same way he greeted everyone—with a smile. Warner said something to him. The coach, still smiling, said something in return.

The locker room was silent as Warner turned and began walking toward his locker.

Hal wanted to glance around at Blaine and Freddie. Were they surprised, or were they expecting Warner? But he kept his eyes on Warner.

Warner stopped and looked around. He found Hal and walked toward him.

Hal waited.

To his astonishment, Warner extended his right hand. Hal took it and they shook.

Beyond Warner, Hal saw Blaine grinning and Freddie giving a thumbs-up sign.

Speaking barely above a whisper, Warner said, "It's not easy being Ralph Stevens's son." Then Warner smiled at Hal and walked over to his locker.

"What'd he say?" Ed asked.

"Nothing."